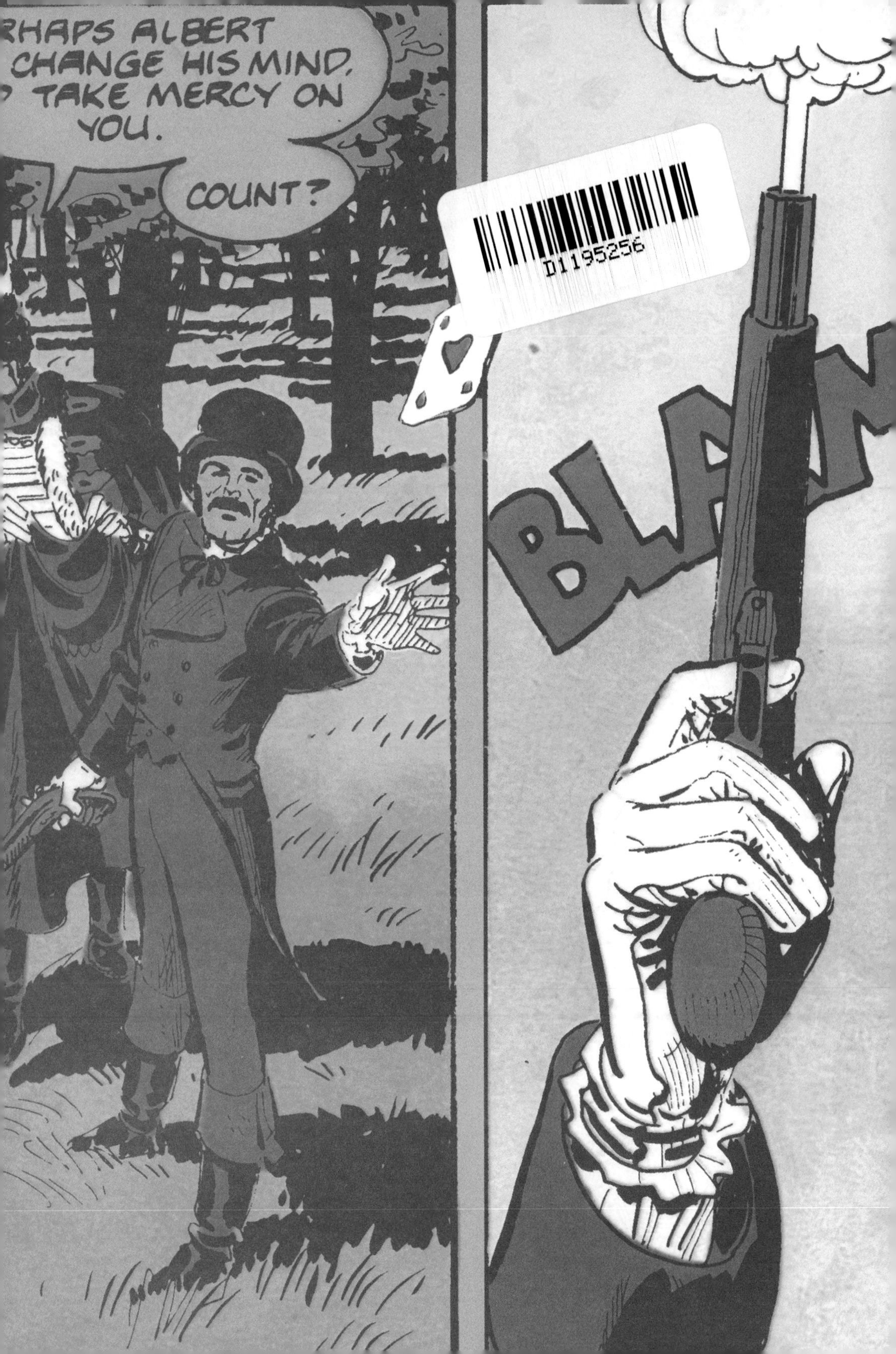
RHAPS ALBERT
CHANGE HIS MIND,
TAKE MERCY ON
YOU.
COUNT?
BLA

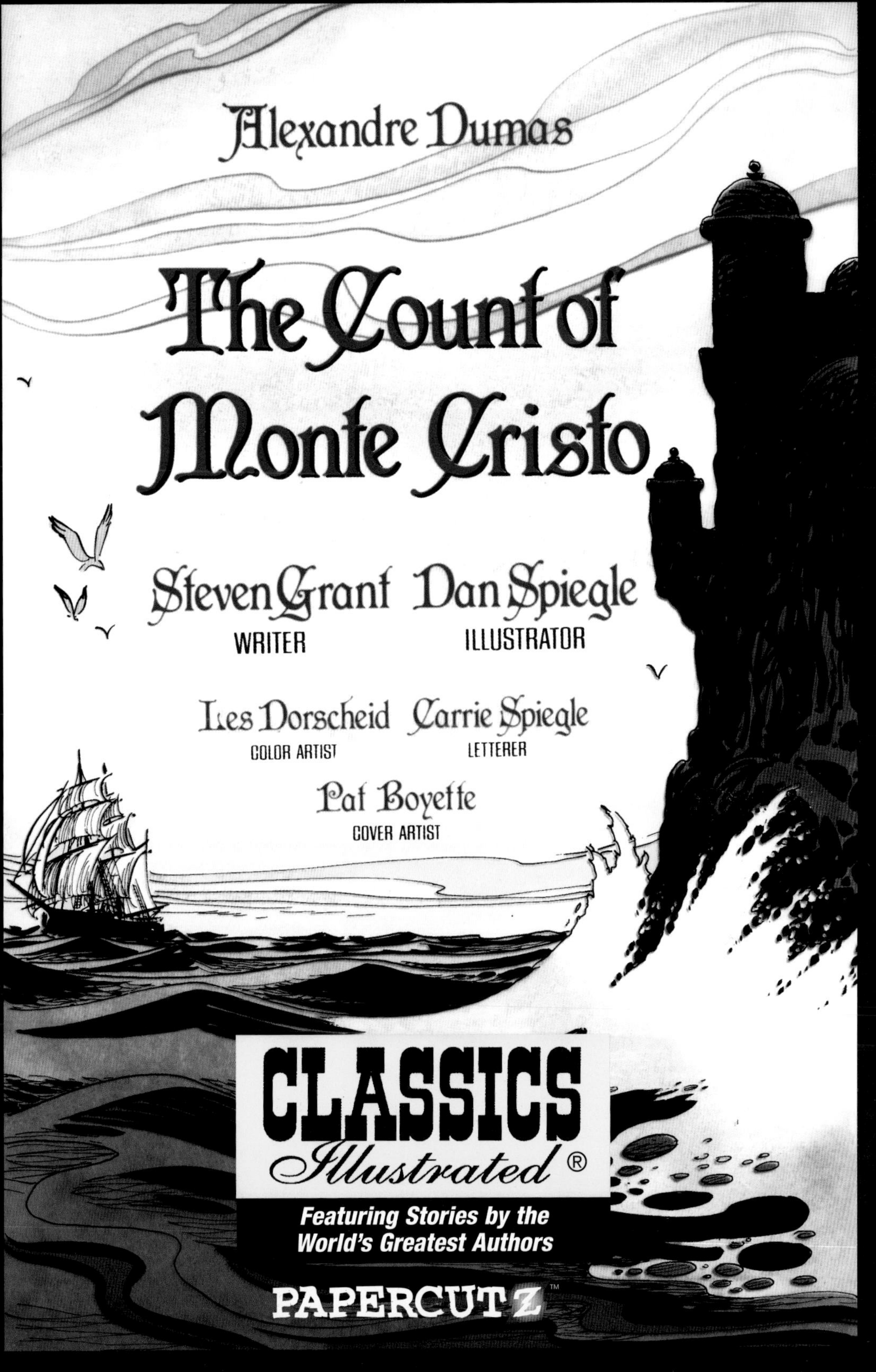

Alexandre Dumas

The Count of Monte Cristo

Steven Grant
WRITER

Dan Spiegle
ILLUSTRATOR

Les Dorscheid
COLOR ARTIST

Carrie Spiegle
LETTERER

Pat Boyette
COVER ARTIST

CLASSICS Illustrated®

Featuring Stories by the World's Greatest Authors

PAPERCUTZ™

CLASSICS ILLUSTRATED GRAPHIC NOVELS AVAILABLE FROM PAPERCUTZ

CLASSICS ILLUSTRATED DELUXE:

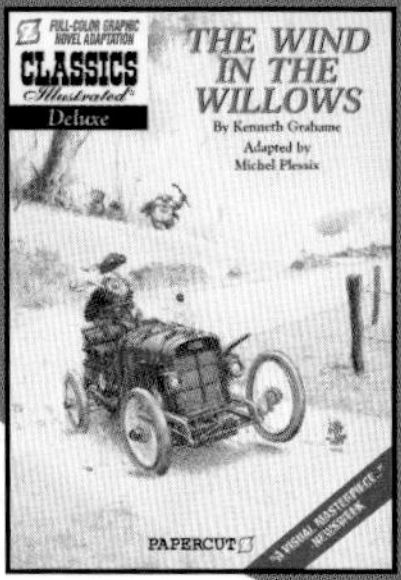
CLASSICS Illustrated Deluxe
THE WIND IN THE WILLOWS
By Kenneth Grahame
Adapted by Michel Plessix
PAPERCUTZ

#1 "The Wind In The Willows"

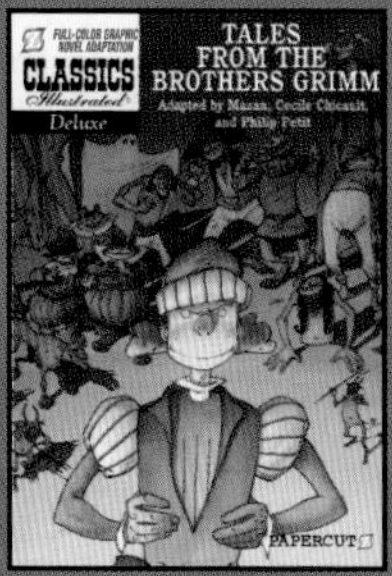
CLASSICS Illustrated Deluxe
TALES FROM THE BROTHERS GRIMM
PAPERCUTZ

#2 "Tales From The Brothers Grimm"

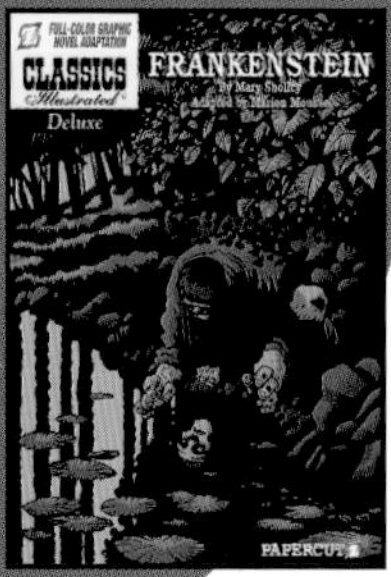
CLASSICS Illustrated Deluxe
FRANKENSTEIN
By Mary Shelley
PAPERCUTZ

#3 "Frankenstein"

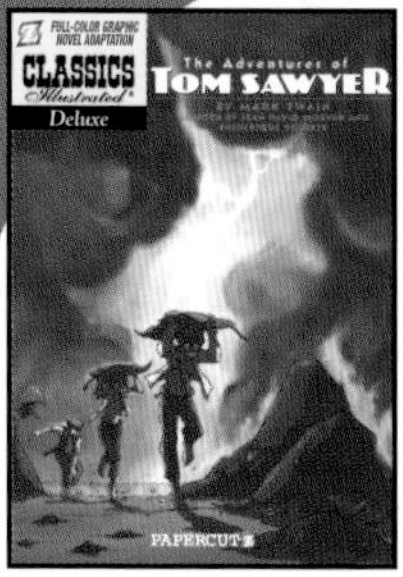
CLASSICS Illustrated Deluxe
The Adventures of TOM SAWYER
BY MARK TWAIN
PAPERCUTZ

#4 "The Adventures of Tom Sawyer"

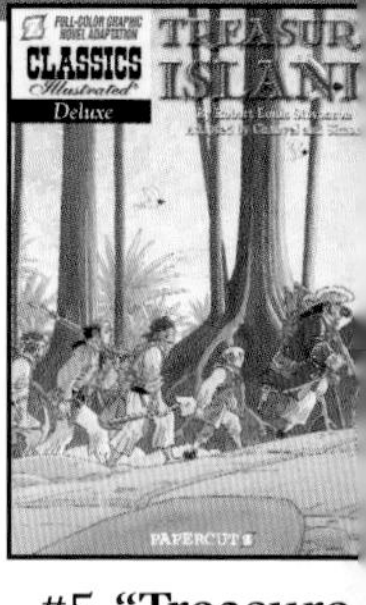
CLASSICS Illustrated Deluxe
PAPERCUTZ

#5 "Treasure Island"

CLASSICS ILLUSTRATED:

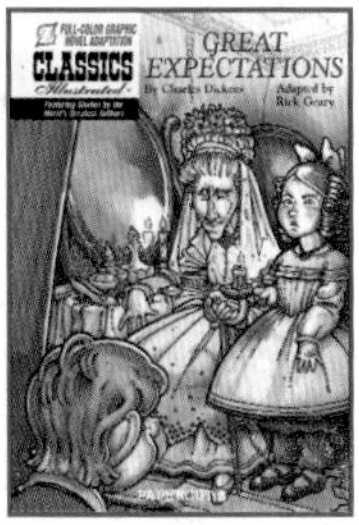
CLASSICS Illustrated
GREAT EXPECTATIONS
By Charles Dickens
Adapted by Rick Geary
PAPERCUTZ

#1 "Great Expectations"

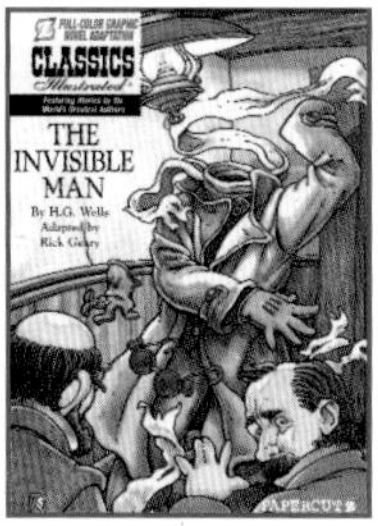
CLASSICS Illustrated
THE INVISIBLE MAN
By H.G. Wells
Adapted by Rick Geary
PAPERCUTZ

#2 "The Invisible Man"

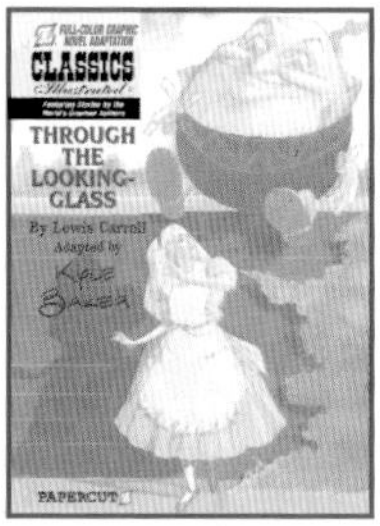
CLASSICS Illustrated
THROUGH THE LOOKING-GLASS
By Lewis Carroll
PAPERCUTZ

#3 "Through the Looking-Glass"

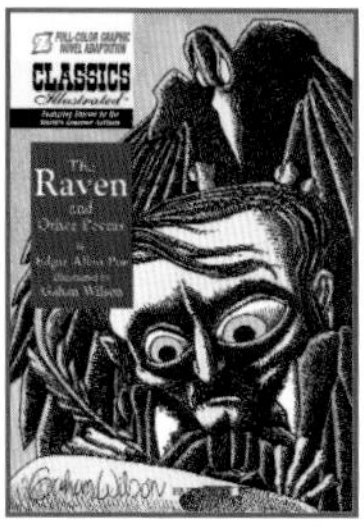
CLASSICS Illustrated
The Raven and Other Poems
Edgar Allan Poe

#4 "The Raven and Other Poems"

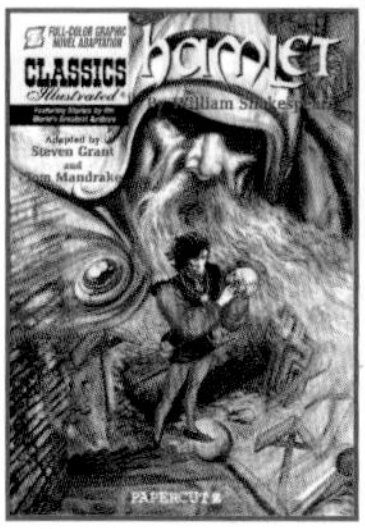
CLASSICS Illustrated
Hamlet
William Shakespeare
Adapted by Steven Grant and Tom Mandrake
PAPERCUTZ

#5 "Hamlet"

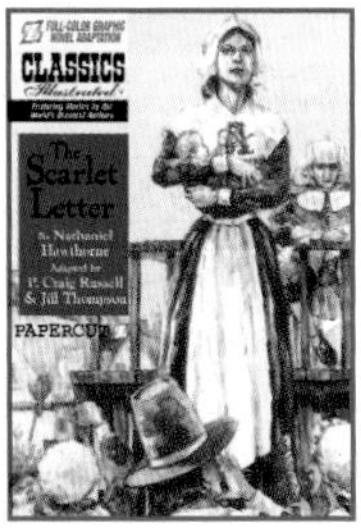
CLASSICS Illustrated
The Scarlet Letter
By Nathaniel Hawthorne
PAPERCUTZ

#6 "The Scarlet Letter"

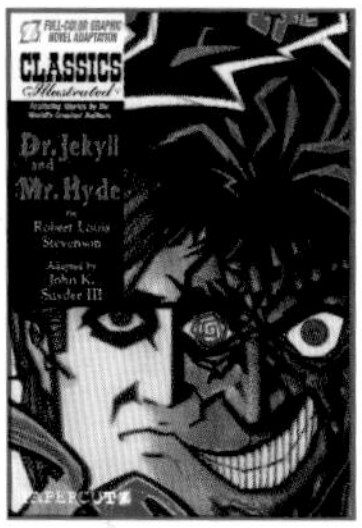
CLASSICS Illustrated
Dr. Jekyll and Mr. Hyde
Robert Louis Stevenson
PAPERCUTZ

#7 "Dr. Jekyll & Mr. Hyde"

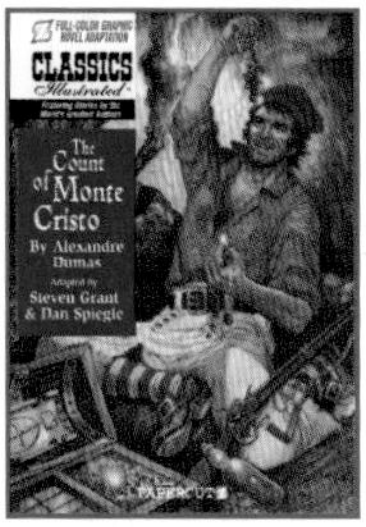
CLASSICS Illustrated
The Count of Monte Cristo
By Alexandre Dumas
Adapted by Steven Grant & Dan Spiegle
PAPERCUTZ

#8 "The Count of Monte Cristo"

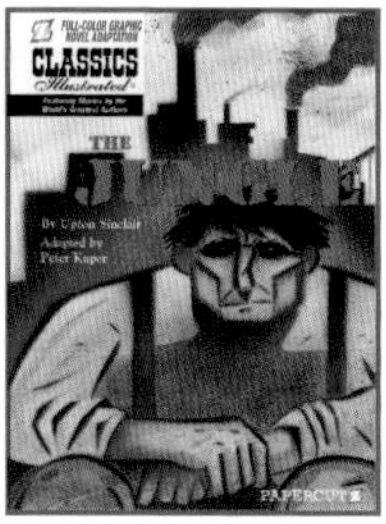
CLASSICS Illustrated
By Upton Sinclair
Adapted by Peter Kuper
PAPERCUTZ

Coming April '10
#9 "The Jungle"

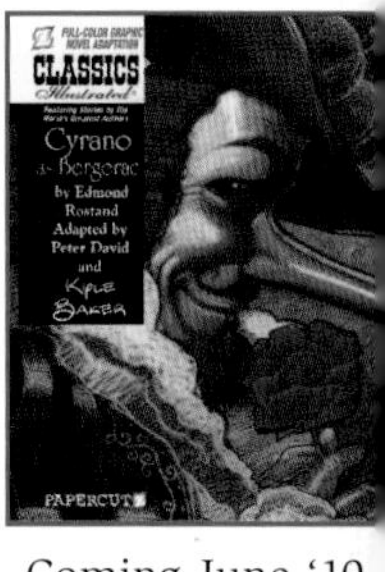
CLASSICS Illustrated
Cyrano de Bergerac
by Edmond Rostand
Adapted by Peter David and Kyle Baker
PAPERCUTZ

Coming June '10
#10 "Cyrano de Bergerac"

Classics Illustrated Deluxe are available for $13.95 each in paperback and $17.95 in hardcover.
Classics Illustrated are available only in hardcover for $9.95 each, except #8, 9, 10, $9.99.
Please add $4.00 for postage and handling for the first book, add $1.00 for each additional book.
MC, Visa, Amex accepted or make check payable to NBM Publishing.
Send to: Papercutz, 40 Exchange Place, Suite 1308, New York, NY 10005 • 1-800-866-1223

WWW.PAPERCUTZ.COM

CLASSICS Illustrated ®

Featuring Stories by the World's Greatest Authors

#8

The Count of Monte Cristo

By Alexandre Dumas
Adapted by Steven Grant
and Dan Spiegle

PAPERCUTZ ™
New York

"What is history?" the great nineteenth-century French author Alexander Dumas once asked. "It is the nail on which I hang my novels." Indeed, the nail on which Dumas hung **The Count of Monte Cristo** involved an actual criminal case. Dumas, "elevating history to the dignity of the novel," fleshed out the real-life narrative, added a number of plot devices (including a hair's-breadth escape, an intriguing mystery, and a number of duels), and created a superb cast of supporting characters. Like several of his other works, the novel was first printed in serialized newspaper installments. By the time **The Count of Monte Cristo** appeared in 1844-45, Dumas was already among France's most popular authors, having perfected his melodramatic style in a series of highly success-ful plays and novels, including *The Three Musketeers*. Although celebrated by the public, **The Count of Monte Cristo** was viewed with disfavor by critics. Certainly, the novel has its literary weaknesses. In addition, his detractors charged Dumas – who often worked with collaborators – with running a novel factory; referring to Dumas's 301 volume *Complete Works*, one critic remarked, "No one has read *all* of Dumas – that would be as impossible as for him to have written it." Since all of his manuscripts are in his own handwriting, however, it is now generally recognized that Dumas's aides provided only research and rough outlines. Later reassessments have muted some of the early criticism and, today, **The Count of Monte Cristo** – as popular with readers as ever – is regard-ed as a spellbinding adventure tale and a window into a dazzling era.

The Count of Monte Cristo
By Alexandre Dumas
Adapted by Steven Grant, writer
Dan Spiegle, artist
Les Dorsheid, colorist
Carrie Spiegle, letterer
Pat Boyette, cover artist
Wade Roberts, Original Editorial Director
Alex Wald, Original Art Director
Production by Ortho
Classics Illustrated Historians — John Haufe and William B. Jones Jr.
Editorial Assistant — Michael Petranek
Jim Salicrup
Editor-in-Chief

ISBN: 978-1-59707-177-2

Printed in Hong Kong
October 2009 by New Era Printing LTD.
Trend Centre, 29-31 Cheung Lee St.
Rm.1101-1103, 11/F
Chaiwan, Hong Kong

Distributed by Macmillan.

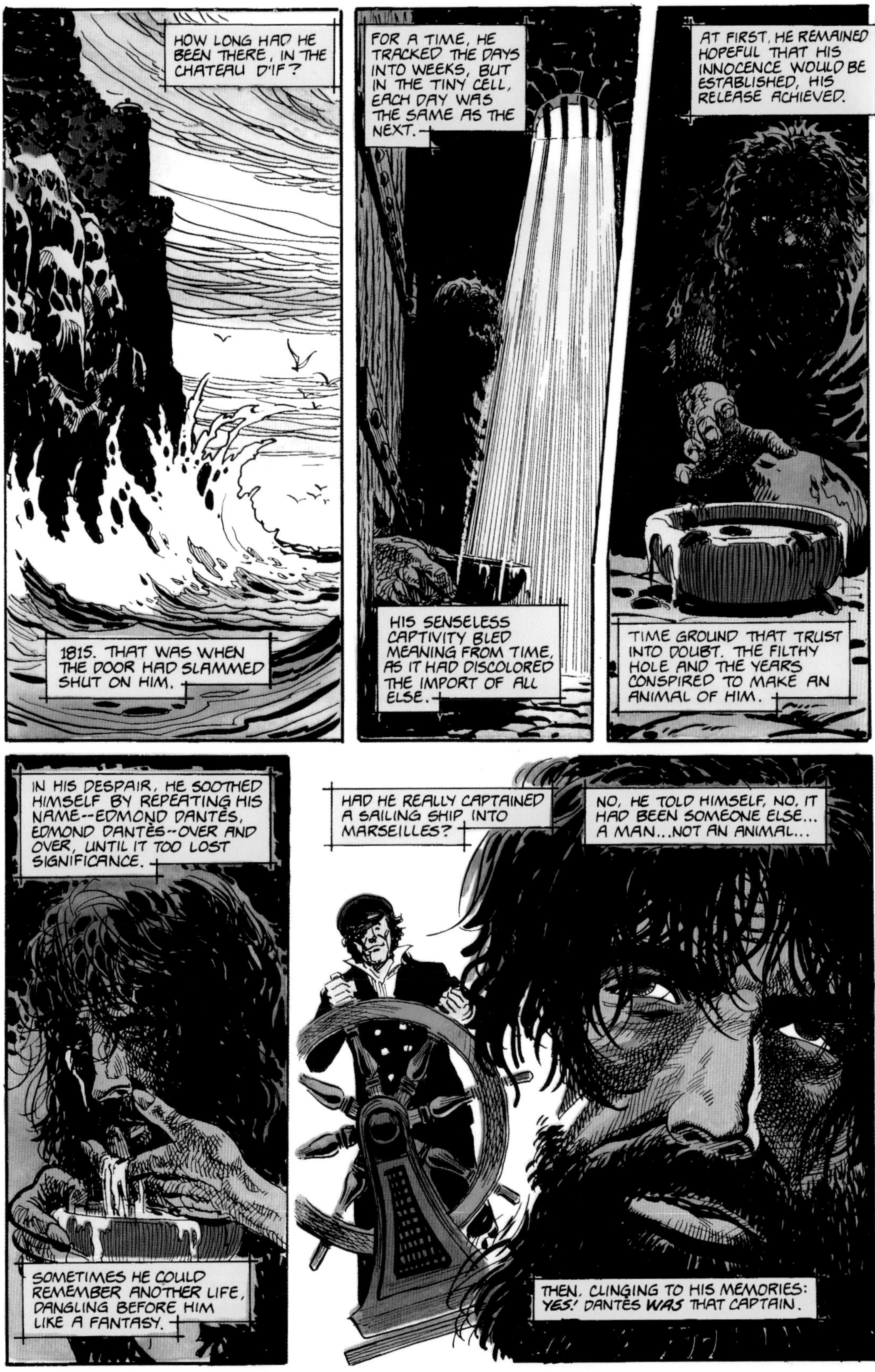
HOW LONG HAD HE BEEN THERE, IN THE CHATEAU D'IF?
1815. THAT WAS WHEN THE DOOR HAD SLAMMED SHUT ON HIM.
FOR A TIME, HE TRACKED THE DAYS INTO WEEKS, BUT IN THE TINY CELL, EACH DAY WAS THE SAME AS THE NEXT.
HIS SENSELESS CAPTIVITY BLED MEANING FROM TIME, AS IT HAD DISCOLORED THE IMPORT OF ALL ELSE.
AT FIRST, HE REMAINED HOPEFUL THAT HIS INNOCENCE WOULD BE ESTABLISHED, HIS RELEASE ACHIEVED.
TIME GROUND THAT TRUST INTO DOUBT. THE FILTHY HOLE AND THE YEARS CONSPIRED TO MAKE AN ANIMAL OF HIM.
IN HIS DESPAIR, HE SOOTHED HIMSELF BY REPEATING HIS NAME--EDMOND DANTÈS, EDMOND DANTÈS--OVER AND OVER, UNTIL IT TOO LOST SIGNIFICANCE.
SOMETIMES HE COULD REMEMBER ANOTHER LIFE, DANGLING BEFORE HIM LIKE A FANTASY.
HAD HE REALLY CAPTAINED A SAILING SHIP INTO MARSEILLES?
NO, HE TOLD HIMSELF, NO, IT HAD BEEN SOMEONE ELSE... A MAN...NOT AN ANIMAL...
THEN, CLINGING TO HIS MEMORIES: *YES!* DANTÈS *WAS* THAT CAPTAIN.

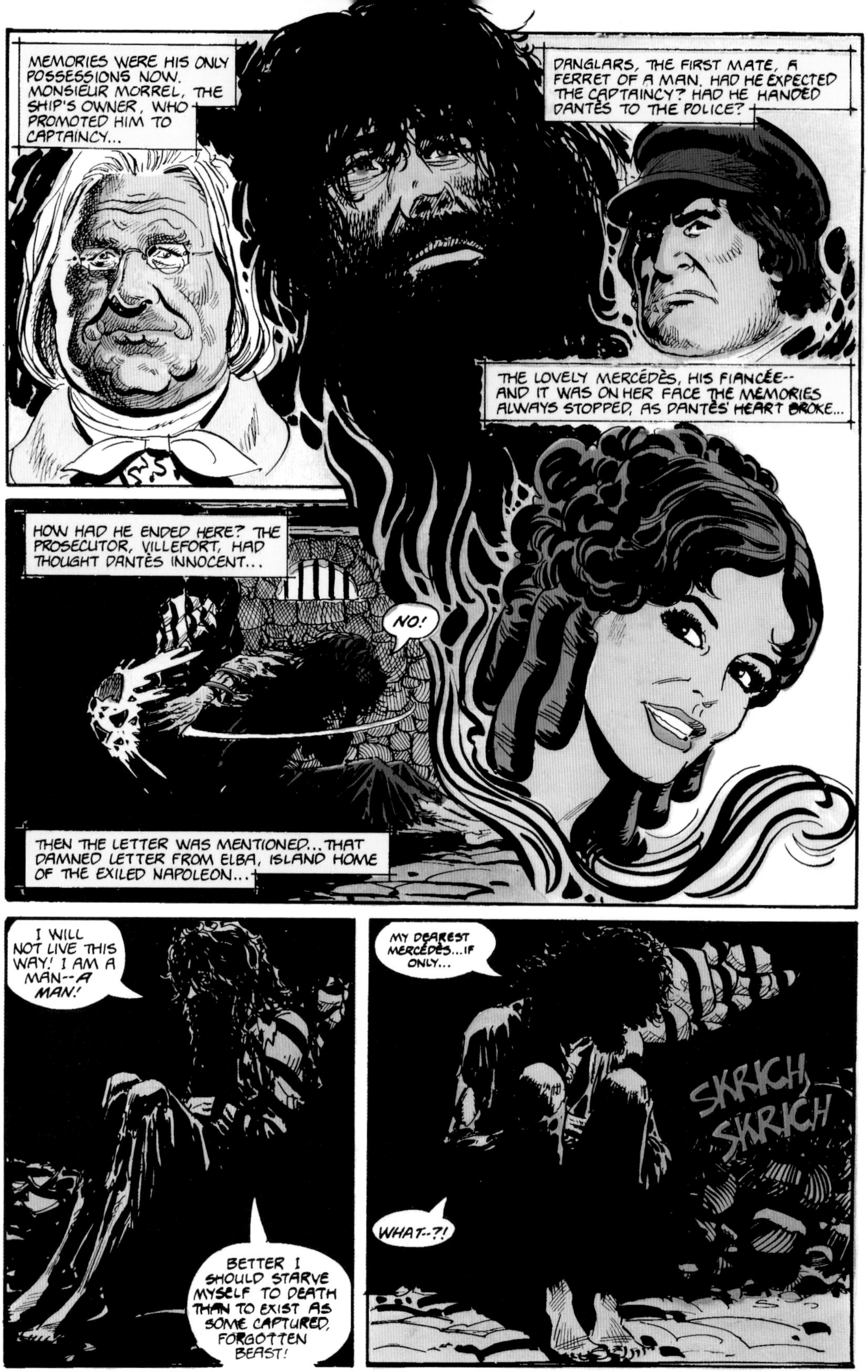
MEMORIES WERE HIS ONLY POSSESSIONS NOW. MONSIEUR MORREL, THE SHIP'S OWNER, WHO PROMOTED HIM TO CAPTAINCY...
DANGLARS, THE FIRST MATE, A FERRET OF A MAN. HAD HE EXPECTED THE CAPTAINCY? HAD HE HANDED DANTÈS TO THE POLICE?
THE LOVELY MERCÉDÈS, HIS FIANCÉE-- AND IT WAS ON HER FACE THE MEMORIES ALWAYS STOPPED, AS DANTÈS' HEART BROKE...
HOW HAD HE ENDED HERE? THE PROSECUTOR, VILLEFORT, HAD THOUGHT DANTÈS INNOCENT...
NO!
THEN THE LETTER WAS MENTIONED... THAT DAMNED LETTER FROM ELBA, ISLAND HOME OF THE EXILED NAPOLEON...
I WILL NOT LIVE THIS WAY! I AM A MAN-- A MAN!
BETTER I SHOULD STARVE MYSELF TO DEATH THAN TO EXIST AS SOME CAPTURED, FORGOTTEN BEAST!
MY DEAREST MERCÉDÈS... IF ONLY...
SKRICH SKRICH
WHAT--?!

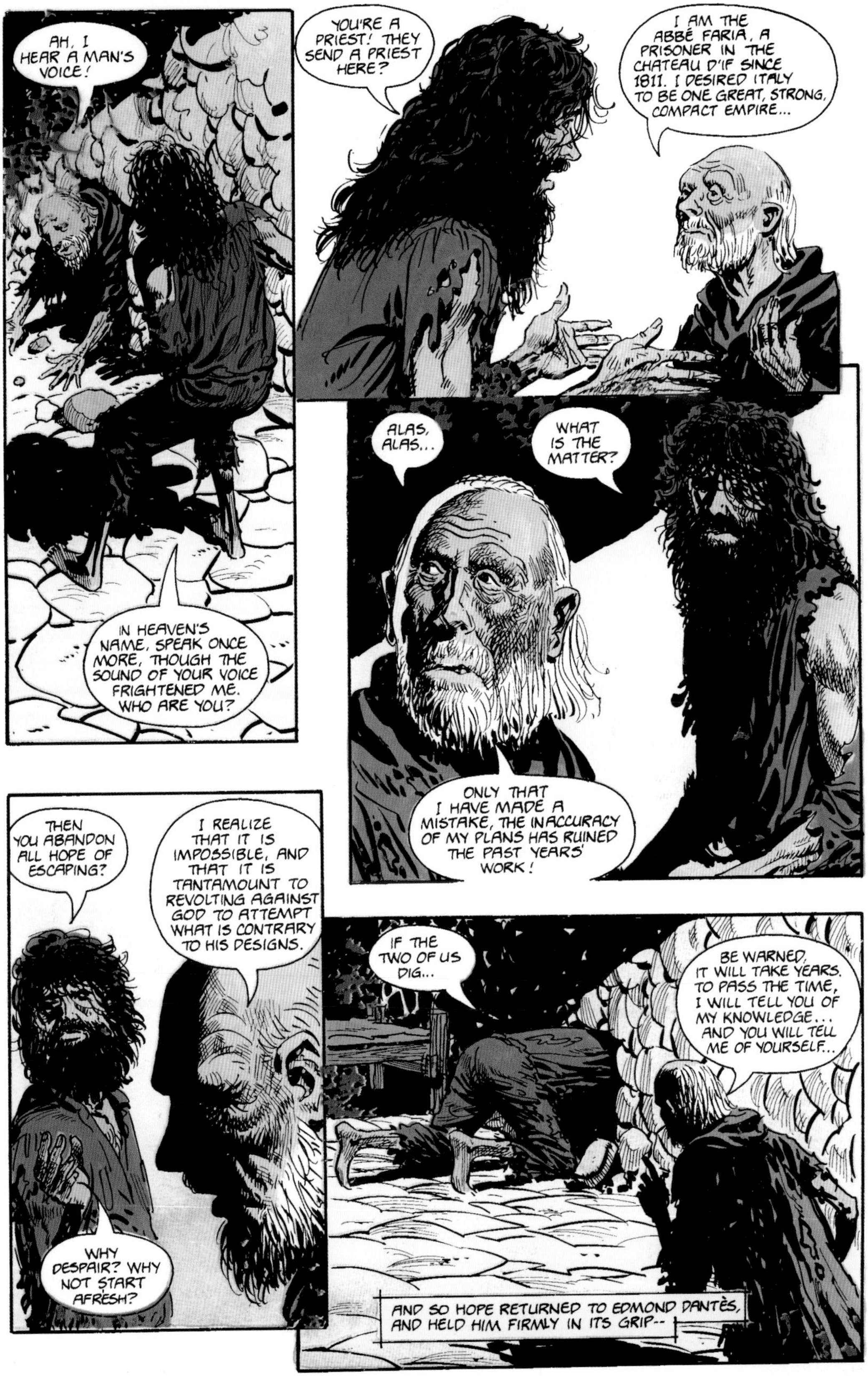
AH, I HEAR A MAN'S VOICE!
IN HEAVEN'S NAME, SPEAK ONCE MORE, THOUGH THE SOUND OF YOUR VOICE FRIGHTENED ME. WHO ARE YOU?
YOU'RE A PRIEST! THEY SEND A PRIEST HERE?
I AM THE ABBÉ FARIA, A PRISONER IN THE CHATEAU D'IF SINCE 1811. I DESIRED ITALY TO BE ONE GREAT, STRONG, COMPACT EMPIRE...
ALAS, ALAS...
WHAT IS THE MATTER?
ONLY THAT I HAVE MADE A MISTAKE, THE INACCURACY OF MY PLANS HAS RUINED THE PAST YEARS' WORK!
THEN YOU ABANDON ALL HOPE OF ESCAPING?
I REALIZE THAT IT IS IMPOSSIBLE, AND THAT IT IS TANTAMOUNT TO REVOLTING AGAINST GOD TO ATTEMPT WHAT IS CONTRARY TO HIS DESIGNS.
WHY DESPAIR? WHY NOT START AFRESH?
IF THE TWO OF US DIG...
BE WARNED, IT WILL TAKE YEARS. TO PASS THE TIME, I WILL TELL YOU OF MY KNOWLEDGE... AND YOU WILL TELL ME OF YOURSELF...
AND SO HOPE RETURNED TO EDMOND DANTÈS, AND HELD HIM FIRMLY IN ITS GRIP--

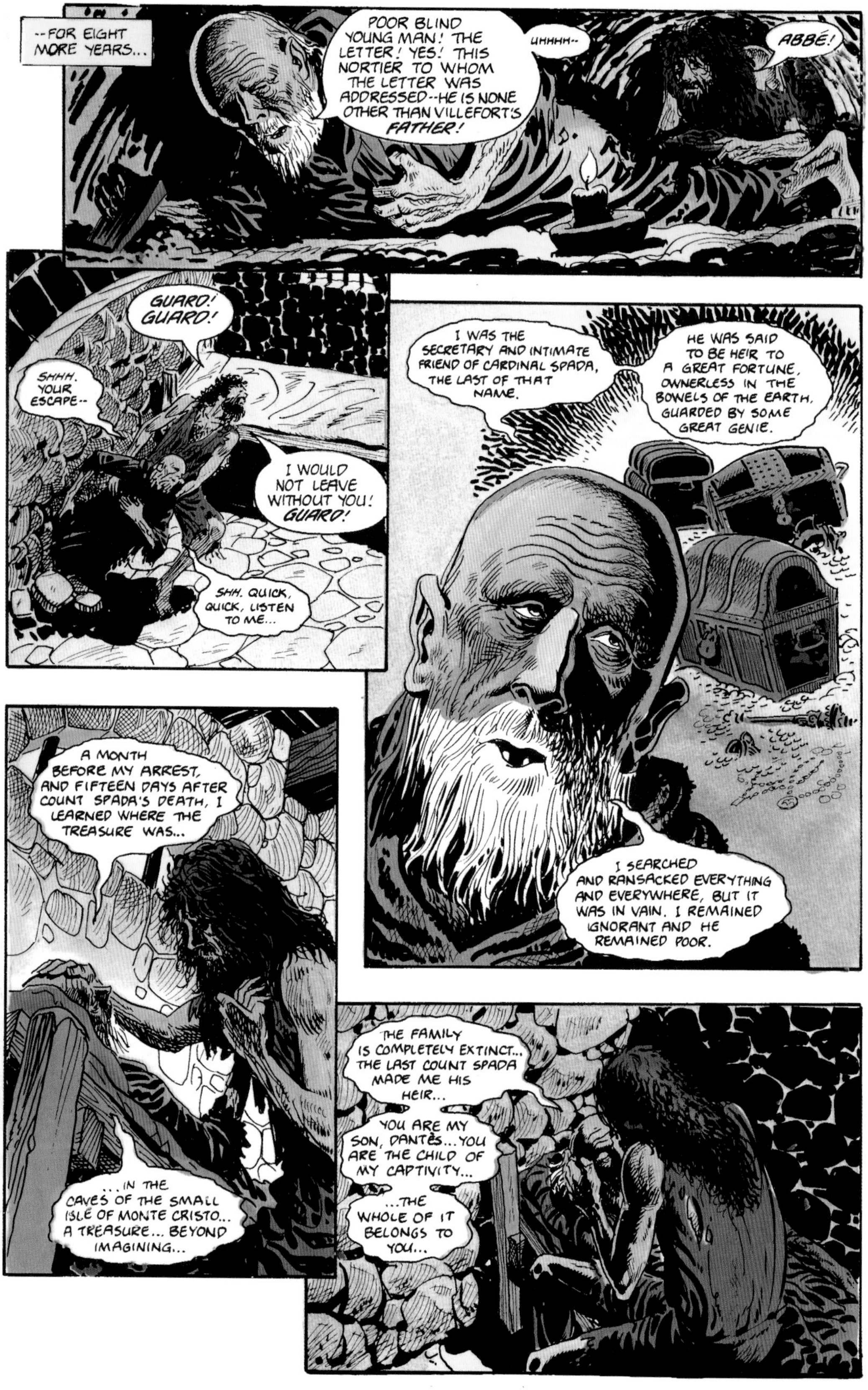
--FOR EIGHT MORE YEARS...
POOR BLIND YOUNG MAN! THE LETTER! YES! THIS NORTIER TO WHOM THE LETTER WAS ADDRESSED--HE IS NONE OTHER THAN VILLEFORT'S FATHER!
UHHHH--
ABBÉ!
GUARD! GUARD!
SHHH. YOUR ESCAPE--
I WOULD NOT LEAVE WITHOUT YOU! GUARD!
SHH. QUICK, QUICK, LISTEN TO ME...
I WAS THE SECRETARY AND INTIMATE FRIEND OF CARDINAL SPADA, THE LAST OF THAT NAME.
HE WAS SAID TO BE HEIR TO A GREAT FORTUNE, OWNERLESS IN THE BOWELS OF THE EARTH, GUARDED BY SOME GREAT GENIE.
I SEARCHED AND RANSACKED EVERYTHING AND EVERYWHERE, BUT IT WAS IN VAIN. I REMAINED IGNORANT AND HE REMAINED POOR.
A MONTH BEFORE MY ARREST, AND FIFTEEN DAYS AFTER COUNT SPADA'S DEATH, I LEARNED WHERE THE TREASURE WAS...
...IN THE CAVES OF THE SMALL ISLE OF MONTE CRISTO... A TREASURE... BEYOND IMAGINING...
THE FAMILY IS COMPLETELY EXTINCT... THE LAST COUNT SPADA MADE ME HIS HEIR...
YOU ARE MY SON, DANTÈS... YOU ARE THE CHILD OF MY CAPTIVITY...
...THE WHOLE OF IT BELONGS TO YOU...

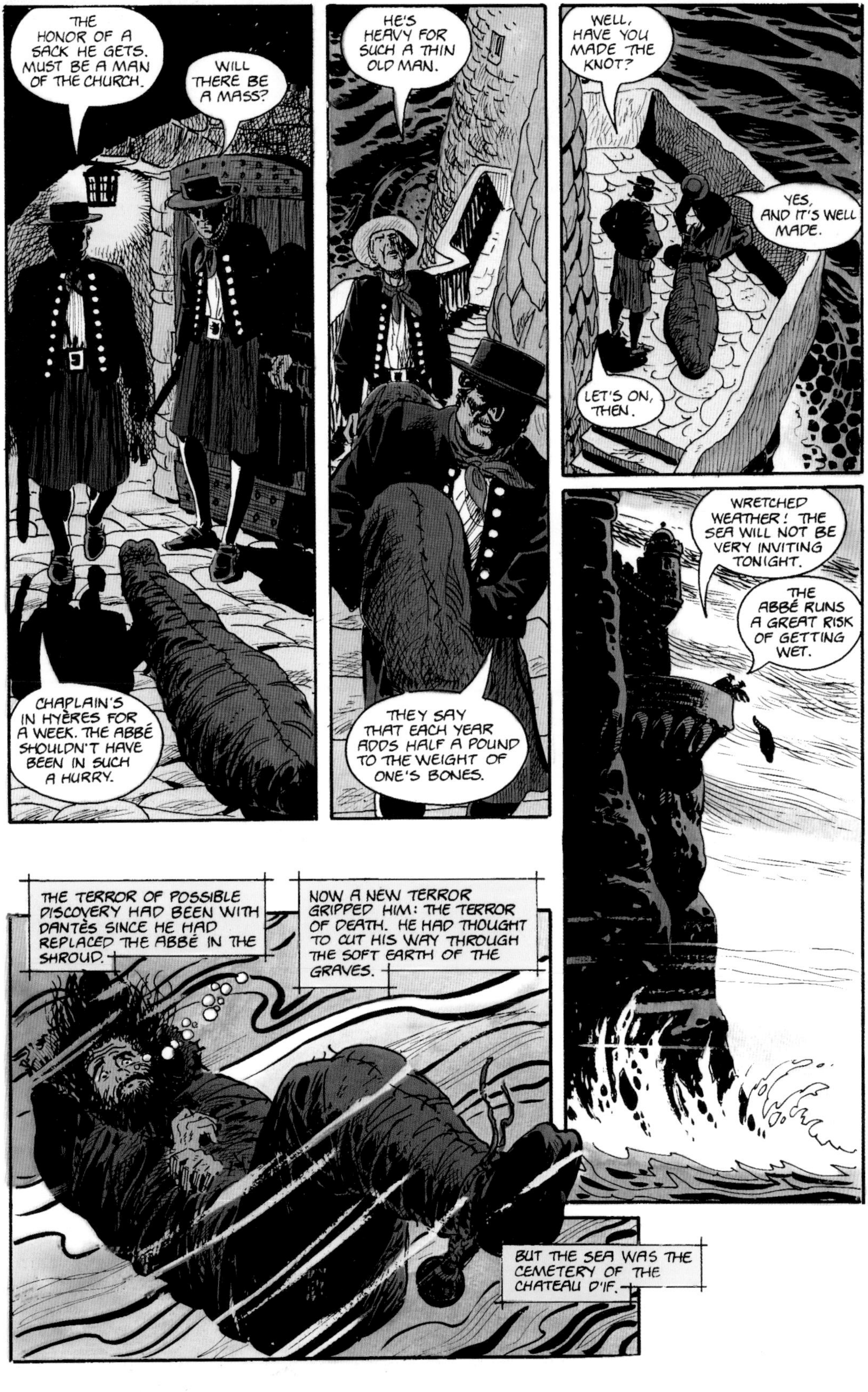
THE HONOR OF A SACK HE GETS. MUST BE A MAN OF THE CHURCH.
WILL THERE BE A MASS?
CHAPLAIN'S IN HYÈRES FOR A WEEK. THE ABBÉ SHOULDN'T HAVE BEEN IN SUCH A HURRY.
HE'S HEAVY FOR SUCH A THIN OLD MAN.
THEY SAY THAT EACH YEAR ADDS HALF A POUND TO THE WEIGHT OF ONE'S BONES.
WELL, HAVE YOU MADE THE KNOT?
YES, AND IT'S WELL MADE.
LET'S ON, THEN.
WRETCHED WEATHER! THE SEA WILL NOT BE VERY INVITING TONIGHT.
THE ABBÉ RUNS A GREAT RISK OF GETTING WET.
THE TERROR OF POSSIBLE DISCOVERY HAD BEEN WITH DANTÈS SINCE HE HAD REPLACED THE ABBÉ IN THE SHROUD.
NOW A NEW TERROR GRIPPED HIM: THE TERROR OF DEATH. HE HAD THOUGHT TO CUT HIS WAY THROUGH THE SOFT EARTH OF THE GRAVES.
BUT THE SEA WAS THE CEMETERY OF THE CHATEAU D'IF.

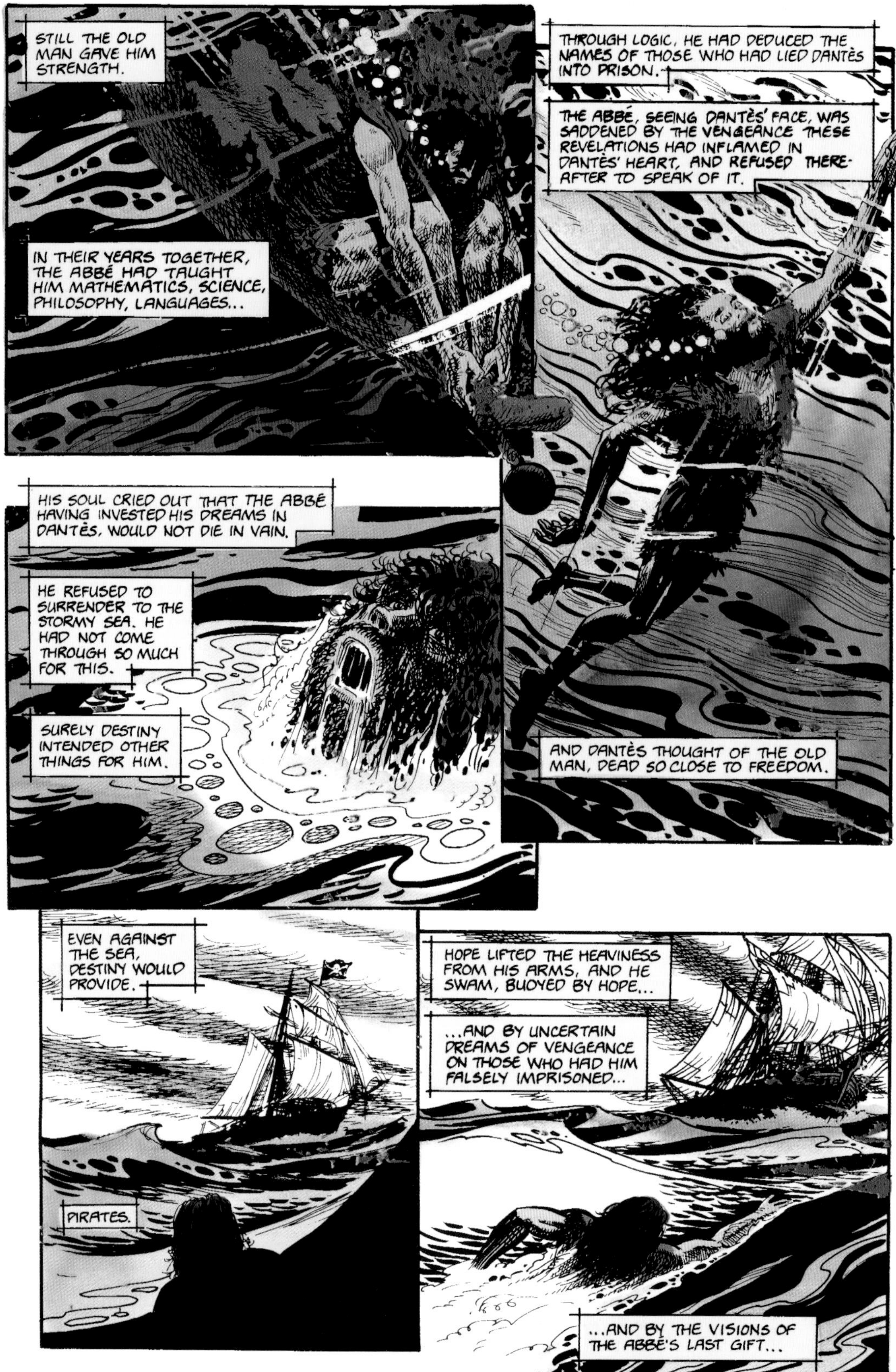
STILL THE OLD MAN GAVE HIM STRENGTH.
IN THEIR YEARS TOGETHER, THE ABBÉ HAD TAUGHT HIM MATHEMATICS, SCIENCE, PHILOSOPHY, LANGUAGES...
THROUGH LOGIC, HE HAD DEDUCED THE NAMES OF THOSE WHO HAD LIED DANTÈS INTO PRISON.
THE ABBÉ, SEEING DANTÈS' FACE, WAS SADDENED BY THE VENGEANCE THESE REVELATIONS HAD INFLAMED IN DANTÈS' HEART, AND REFUSED THEREAFTER TO SPEAK OF IT.
AND DANTÈS THOUGHT OF THE OLD MAN, DEAD SO CLOSE TO FREEDOM.
HIS SOUL CRIED OUT THAT THE ABBÉ HAVING INVESTED HIS DREAMS IN DANTÈS, WOULD NOT DIE IN VAIN.
HE REFUSED TO SURRENDER TO THE STORMY SEA. HE HAD NOT COME THROUGH SO MUCH FOR THIS.
SURELY DESTINY INTENDED OTHER THINGS FOR HIM.
EVEN AGAINST THE SEA, DESTINY WOULD PROVIDE.
PIRATES.
HOPE LIFTED THE HEAVINESS FROM HIS ARMS, AND HE SWAM, BUOYED BY HOPE...
...AND BY UNCERTAIN DREAMS OF VENGEANCE ON THOSE WHO HAD HIM FALSELY IMPRISONED...
...AND BY THE VISIONS OF THE ABBÉ'S LAST GIFT...

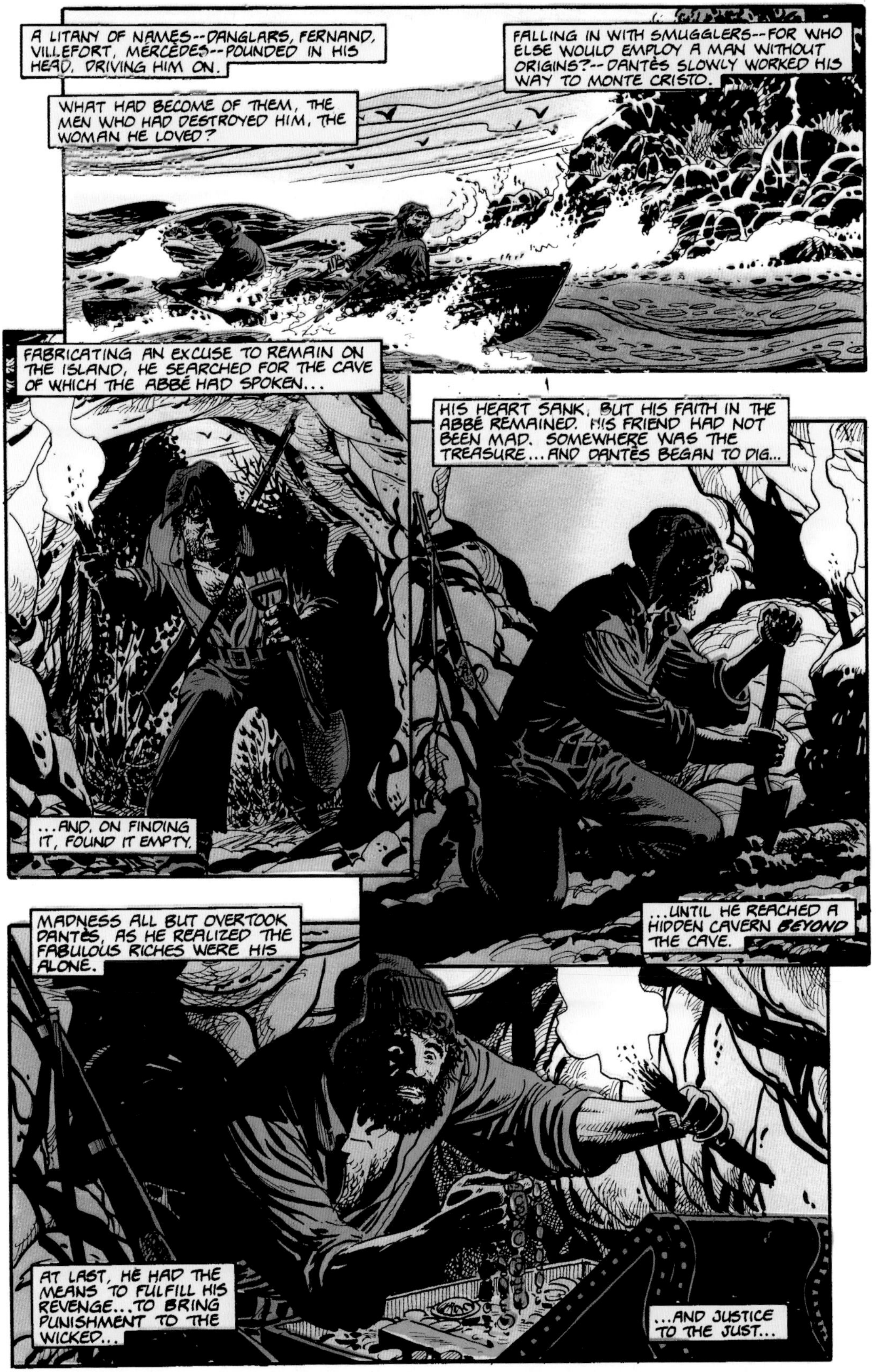
A LITANY OF NAMES--DANGLARS, FERNAND, VILLEFORT, MERCÉDÈS--POUNDED IN HIS HEAD, DRIVING HIM ON.
WHAT HAD BECOME OF THEM, THE MEN WHO HAD DESTROYED HIM, THE WOMAN HE LOVED?
FALLING IN WITH SMUGGLERS--FOR WHO ELSE WOULD EMPLOY A MAN WITHOUT ORIGINS?--DANTÈS SLOWLY WORKED HIS WAY TO MONTE CRISTO.
FABRICATING AN EXCUSE TO REMAIN ON THE ISLAND, HE SEARCHED FOR THE CAVE OF WHICH THE ABBÉ HAD SPOKEN...
...AND, ON FINDING IT, FOUND IT EMPTY.
HIS HEART SANK, BUT HIS FAITH IN THE ABBÉ REMAINED. HIS FRIEND HAD NOT BEEN MAD. SOMEWHERE WAS THE TREASURE... AND DANTÈS BEGAN TO DIG...
...UNTIL HE REACHED A HIDDEN CAVERN *BEYOND* THE CAVE.
MADNESS ALL BUT OVERTOOK DANTÈS, AS HE REALIZED THE FABULOUS RICHES WERE HIS ALONE.
AT LAST, HE HAD THE MEANS TO FULFILL HIS REVENGE... TO BRING PUNISHMENT TO THE WICKED...
...AND JUSTICE TO THE JUST...

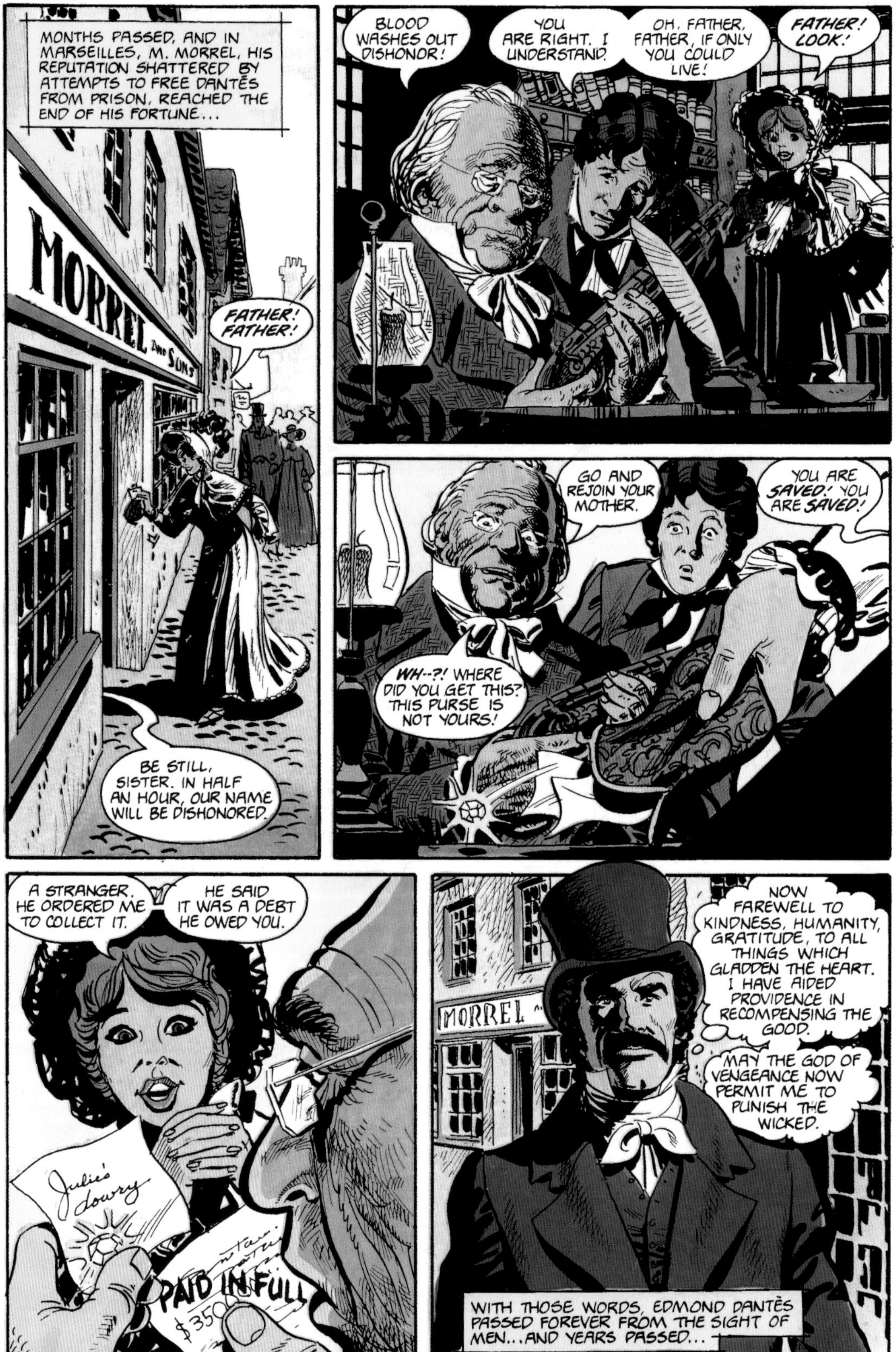

MONTHS PASSED, AND IN MARSEILLES, M. MORREL, HIS REPUTATION SHATTERED BY ATTEMPTS TO FREE DANTÈS FROM PRISON, REACHED THE END OF HIS FORTUNE...
MORREL AND SONS
FATHER! FATHER!
BE STILL, SISTER. IN HALF AN HOUR, OUR NAME WILL BE DISHONORED.
BLOOD WASHES OUT DISHONOR!
YOU ARE RIGHT. I UNDERSTAND.
OH, FATHER, FATHER, IF ONLY YOU COULD LIVE!
FATHER! LOOK!
GO AND REJOIN YOUR MOTHER.
YOU ARE SAVED! YOU ARE SAVED!
WH--?! WHERE DID YOU GET THIS? THIS PURSE IS NOT YOURS!
A STRANGER. HE ORDERED ME TO COLLECT IT.
HE SAID IT WAS A DEBT HE OWED YOU.
Julie's dowry
PAID IN FULL
NOW FAREWELL TO KINDNESS, HUMANITY, GRATITUDE, TO ALL THINGS WHICH GLADDEN THE HEART. I HAVE AIDED PROVIDENCE IN RECOMPENSING THE GOOD.
MAY THE GOD OF VENGEANCE NOW PERMIT ME TO PUNISH THE WICKED.
MORREL
WITH THOSE WORDS, EDMOND DANTÈS PASSED FOREVER FROM THE SIGHT OF MEN...AND YEARS PASSED...

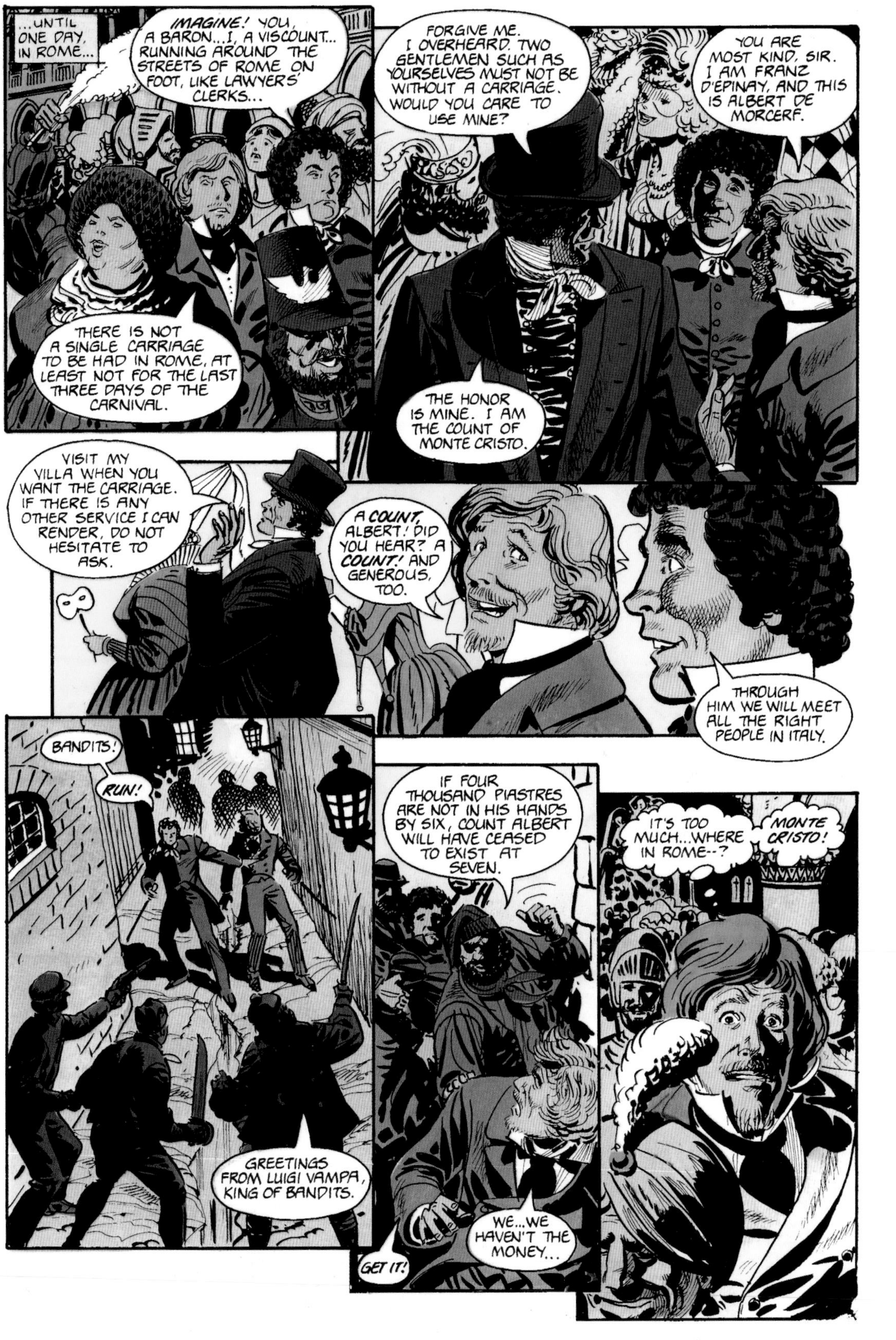
...UNTIL ONE DAY, IN ROME...
IMAGINE! YOU, A BARON...I, A VISCOUNT... RUNNING AROUND THE STREETS OF ROME ON FOOT, LIKE LAWYERS' CLERKS...
THERE IS NOT A SINGLE CARRIAGE TO BE HAD IN ROME, AT LEAST NOT FOR THE LAST THREE DAYS OF THE CARNIVAL.
FORGIVE ME. I OVERHEARD. TWO GENTLEMEN SUCH AS YOURSELVES MUST NOT BE WITHOUT A CARRIAGE. WOULD YOU CARE TO USE MINE?
YOU ARE MOST KIND, SIR. I AM FRANZ D'EPINAY, AND THIS IS ALBERT DE MORCERF.
THE HONOR IS MINE. I AM THE COUNT OF MONTE CRISTO.
VISIT MY VILLA WHEN YOU WANT THE CARRIAGE. IF THERE IS ANY OTHER SERVICE I CAN RENDER, DO NOT HESITATE TO ASK.
A COUNT, ALBERT! DID YOU HEAR? A COUNT! AND GENEROUS, TOO.
THROUGH HIM WE WILL MEET ALL THE RIGHT PEOPLE IN ITALY.
BANDITS!
RUN!
GREETINGS FROM LUIGI VAMPA, KING OF BANDITS.
IF FOUR THOUSAND PIASTRES ARE NOT IN HIS HANDS BY SIX, COUNT ALBERT WILL HAVE CEASED TO EXIST AT SEVEN.
WE...WE HAVEN'T THE MONEY...
GET IT!
IT'S TOO MUCH...WHERE IN ROME--?
MONTE CRISTO!

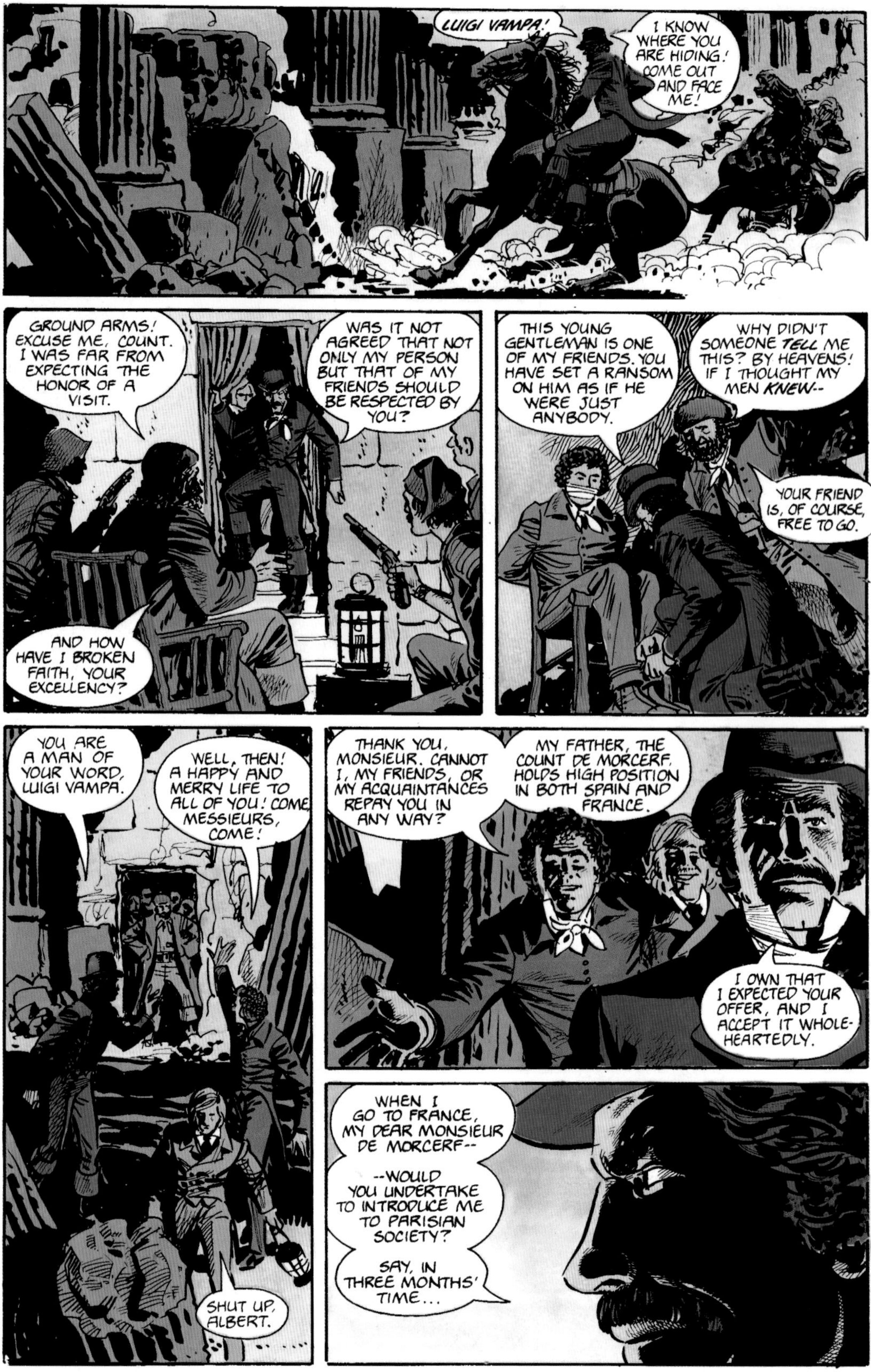
LUIGI VAMPA!
I KNOW WHERE YOU ARE HIDING! COME OUT AND FACE ME!
GROUND ARMS! EXCUSE ME, COUNT. I WAS FAR FROM EXPECTING THE HONOR OF A VISIT.
WAS IT NOT AGREED THAT NOT ONLY MY PERSON BUT THAT OF MY FRIENDS SHOULD BE RESPECTED BY YOU?
AND HOW HAVE I BROKEN FAITH, YOUR EXCELLENCY?
THIS YOUNG GENTLEMAN IS ONE OF MY FRIENDS. YOU HAVE SET A RANSOM ON HIM AS IF HE WERE JUST ANYBODY.
WHY DIDN'T SOMEONE TELL ME THIS? BY HEAVENS! IF I THOUGHT MY MEN KNEW--
YOUR FRIEND IS, OF COURSE, FREE TO GO.
YOU ARE A MAN OF YOUR WORD, LUIGI VAMPA.
WELL, THEN! A HAPPY AND MERRY LIFE TO ALL OF YOU! COME, MESSIEURS, COME!
SHUT UP, ALBERT.
THANK YOU, MONSIEUR. CANNOT I, MY FRIENDS, OR MY ACQUAINTANCES REPAY YOU IN ANY WAY?
MY FATHER, THE COUNT DE MORCERF, HOLDS HIGH POSITION IN BOTH SPAIN AND FRANCE.
I OWN THAT I EXPECTED YOUR OFFER, AND I ACCEPT IT WHOLE-HEARTEDLY.
WHEN I GO TO FRANCE, MY DEAR MONSIEUR DE MORCERF--
--WOULD YOU UNDERTAKE TO INTRODUCE ME TO PARISIAN SOCIETY?
SAY, IN THREE MONTHS' TIME...

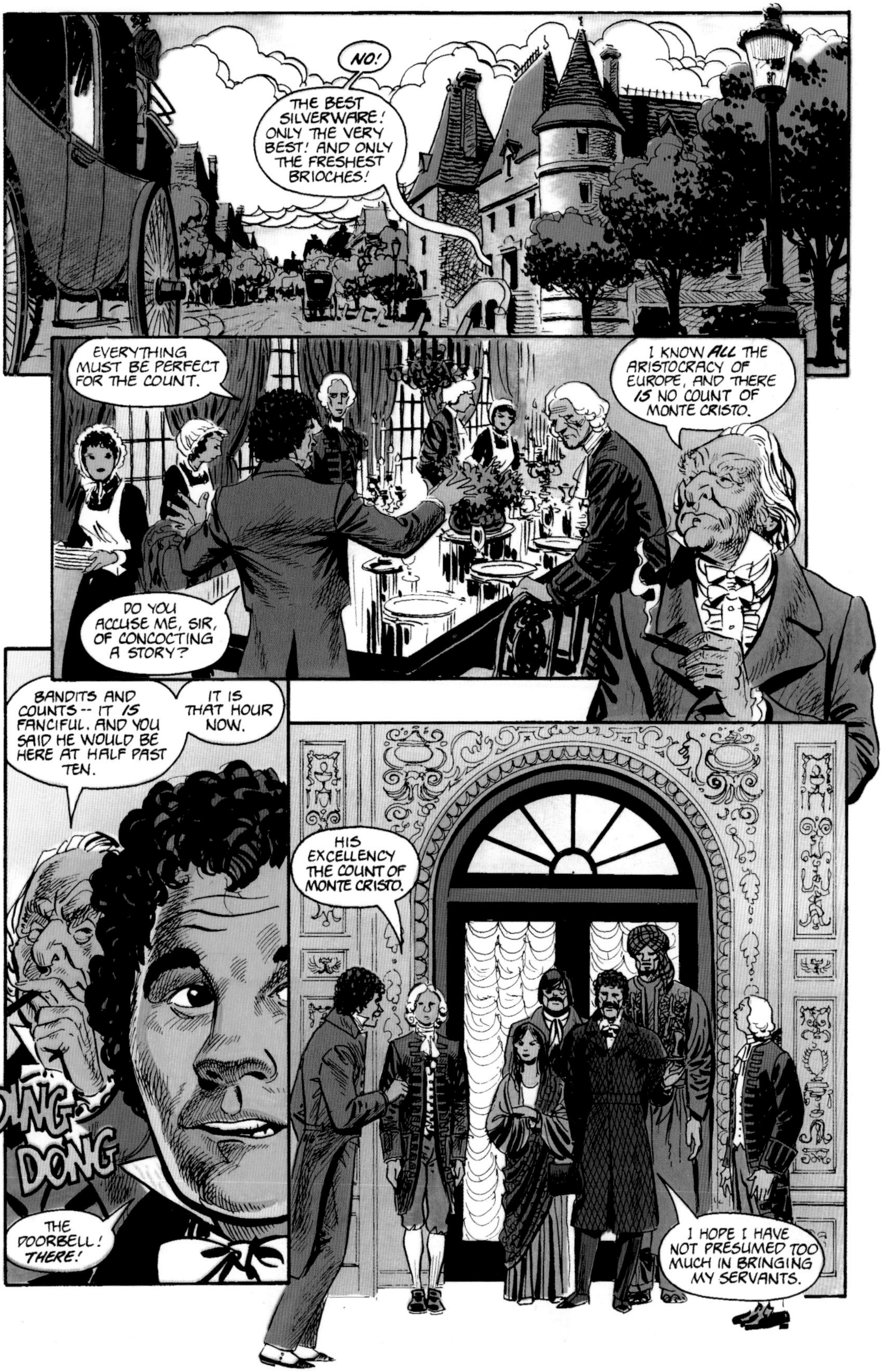
NO!
THE BEST SILVERWARE! ONLY THE VERY BEST! AND ONLY THE FRESHEST BRIOCHES!
EVERYTHING MUST BE PERFECT FOR THE COUNT.
I KNOW ALL THE ARISTOCRACY OF EUROPE, AND THERE IS NO COUNT OF MONTE CRISTO.
DO YOU ACCUSE ME, SIR, OF CONCOCTING A STORY?
BANDITS AND COUNTS -- IT IS FANCIFUL. AND YOU SAID HE WOULD BE HERE AT HALF PAST TEN.
IT IS THAT HOUR NOW.
DING DONG
THE DOORBELL! THERE!
HIS EXCELLENCY THE COUNT OF MONTE CRISTO.
I HOPE I HAVE NOT PRESUMED TOO MUCH IN BRINGING MY SERVANTS.

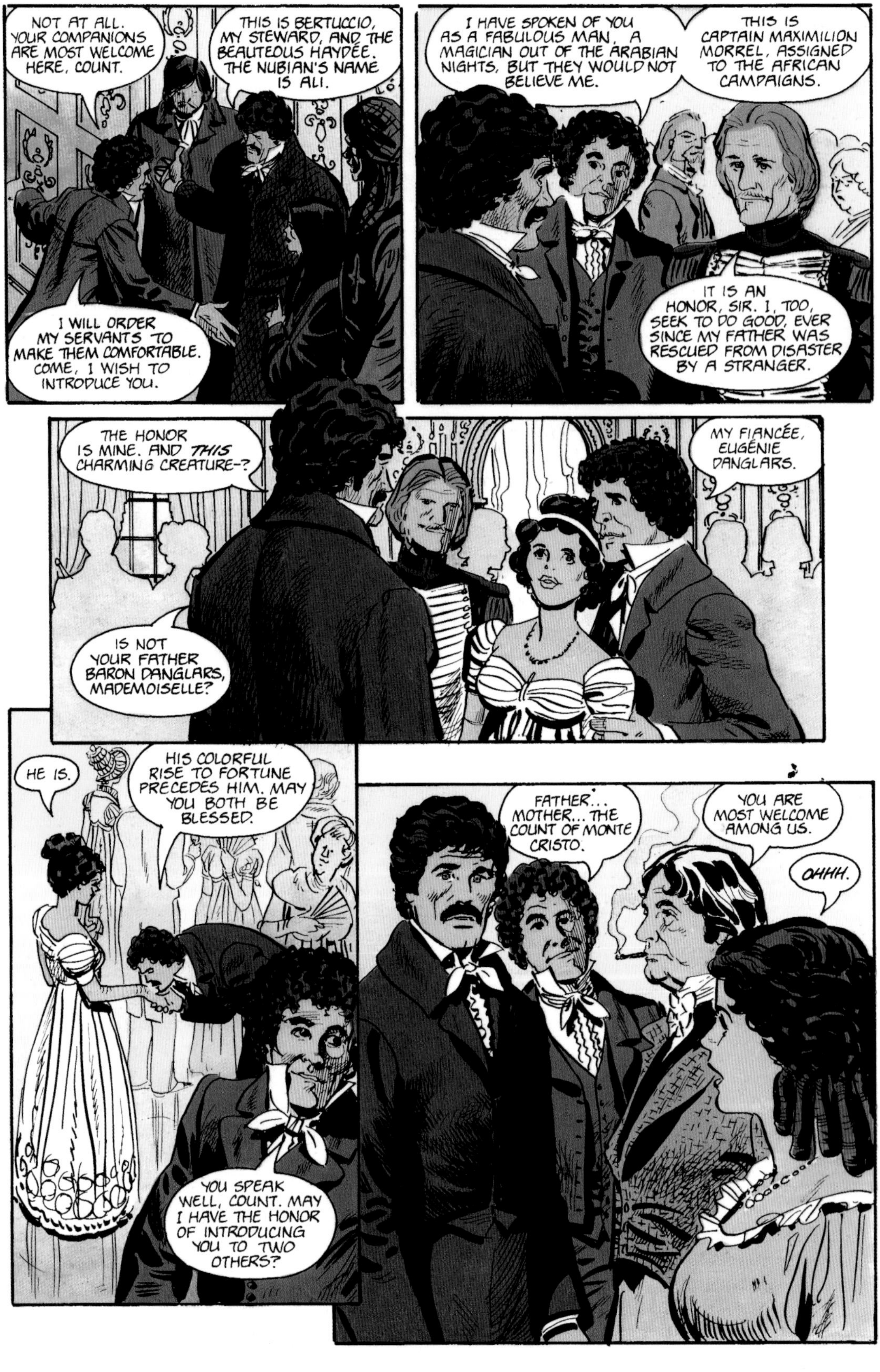

NOT AT ALL. YOUR COMPANIONS ARE MOST WELCOME HERE, COUNT.
THIS IS BERTUCCIO, MY STEWARD, AND THE BEAUTEOUS HAYDÉE. THE NUBIAN'S NAME IS ALI.
I WILL ORDER MY SERVANTS TO MAKE THEM COMFORTABLE. COME, I WISH TO INTRODUCE YOU.
I HAVE SPOKEN OF YOU AS A FABULOUS MAN, A MAGICIAN OUT OF THE ARABIAN NIGHTS, BUT THEY WOULD NOT BELIEVE ME.
THIS IS CAPTAIN MAXIMILION MORREL, ASSIGNED TO THE AFRICAN CAMPAIGNS.
IT IS AN HONOR, SIR. I, TOO, SEEK TO DO GOOD, EVER SINCE MY FATHER WAS RESCUED FROM DISASTER BY A STRANGER.
THE HONOR IS MINE. AND THIS CHARMING CREATURE–?
MY FIANCÉE, EUGÉNIE DANGLARS.
IS NOT YOUR FATHER BARON DANGLARS, MADEMOISELLE?
HE IS.
HIS COLORFUL RISE TO FORTUNE PRECEDES HIM. MAY YOU BOTH BE BLESSED.
YOU SPEAK WELL, COUNT. MAY I HAVE THE HONOR OF INTRODUCING YOU TO TWO OTHERS?
FATHER... MOTHER... THE COUNT OF MONTE CRISTO.
YOU ARE MOST WELCOME AMONG US.
OHHH.

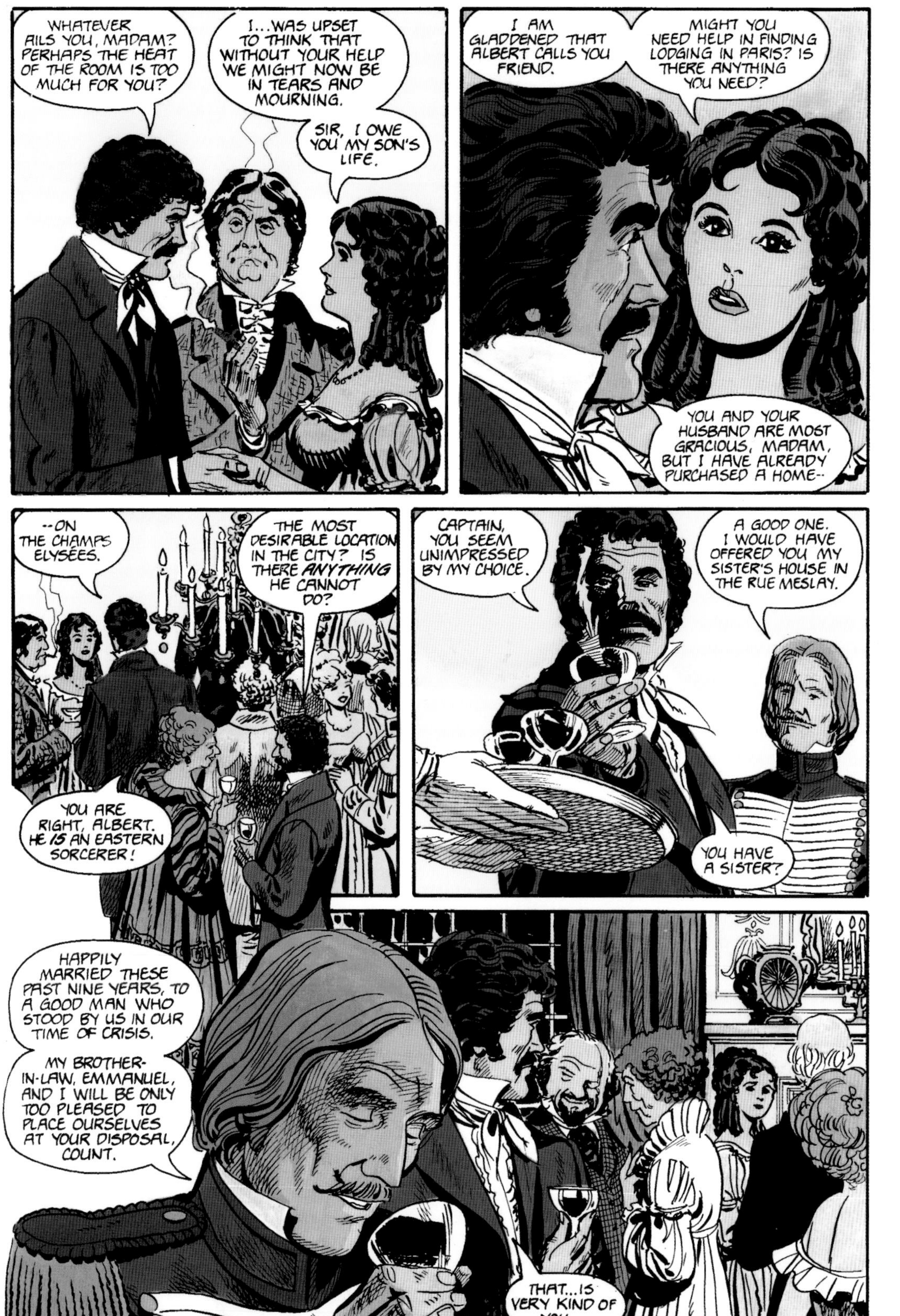
WHATEVER AILS YOU, MADAM? PERHAPS THE HEAT OF THE ROOM IS TOO MUCH FOR YOU?
I...WAS UPSET TO THINK THAT WITHOUT YOUR HELP WE MIGHT NOW BE IN TEARS AND MOURNING.
SIR, I OWE YOU MY SON'S LIFE.
I AM GLADDENED THAT ALBERT CALLS YOU FRIEND.
MIGHT YOU NEED HELP IN FINDING LODGING IN PARIS? IS THERE ANYTHING YOU NEED?
YOU AND YOUR HUSBAND ARE MOST GRACIOUS, MADAM, BUT I HAVE ALREADY PURCHASED A HOME--
--ON THE CHAMPS ELYSÉES.
THE MOST DESIRABLE LOCATION IN THE CITY? IS THERE *ANYTHING* HE CANNOT DO?
YOU ARE RIGHT, ALBERT. HE *IS* AN EASTERN SORCERER!
CAPTAIN, YOU SEEM UNIMPRESSED BY MY CHOICE.
A GOOD ONE. I WOULD HAVE OFFERED YOU MY SISTER'S HOUSE IN THE RUE MESLAY.
YOU HAVE A SISTER?
HAPPILY MARRIED THESE PAST NINE YEARS, TO A GOOD MAN WHO STOOD BY US IN OUR TIME OF CRISIS.
MY BROTHER-IN-LAW, EMMANUEL, AND I WILL BE ONLY TOO PLEASED TO PLACE OURSELVES AT YOUR DISPOSAL, COUNT.
THAT...IS VERY KIND OF YOU...

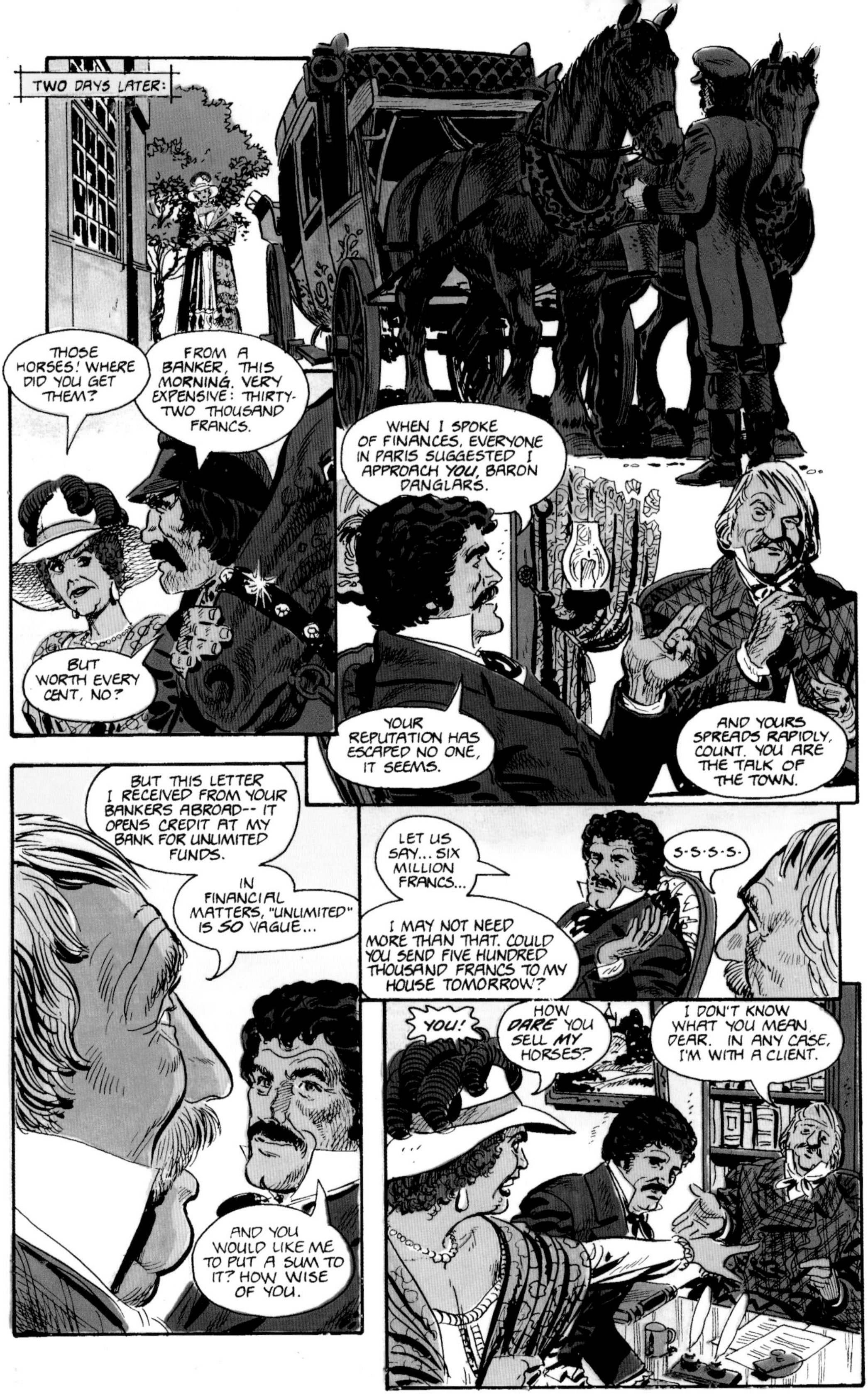
TWO DAYS LATER:
THOSE HORSES! WHERE DID YOU GET THEM?
FROM A BANKER, THIS MORNING. VERY EXPENSIVE: THIRTY-TWO THOUSAND FRANCS.
BUT WORTH EVERY CENT, NO?
WHEN I SPOKE OF FINANCES, EVERYONE IN PARIS SUGGESTED I APPROACH YOU, BARON DANGLARS.
YOUR REPUTATION HAS ESCAPED NO ONE, IT SEEMS.
AND YOURS SPREADS RAPIDLY, COUNT. YOU ARE THE TALK OF THE TOWN.
BUT THIS LETTER I RECEIVED FROM YOUR BANKERS ABROAD-- IT OPENS CREDIT AT MY BANK FOR UNLIMITED FUNDS.
IN FINANCIAL MATTERS, "UNLIMITED" IS SO VAGUE...
AND YOU WOULD LIKE ME TO PUT A SUM TO IT? HOW WISE OF YOU.
LET US SAY... SIX MILLION FRANCS...
S-S-S-S.
I MAY NOT NEED MORE THAN THAT. COULD YOU SEND FIVE HUNDRED THOUSAND FRANCS TO MY HOUSE TOMORROW?
YOU!
HOW DARE YOU SELL MY HORSES?
I DON'T KNOW WHAT YOU MEAN, DEAR. IN ANY CASE, I'M WITH A CLIENT.

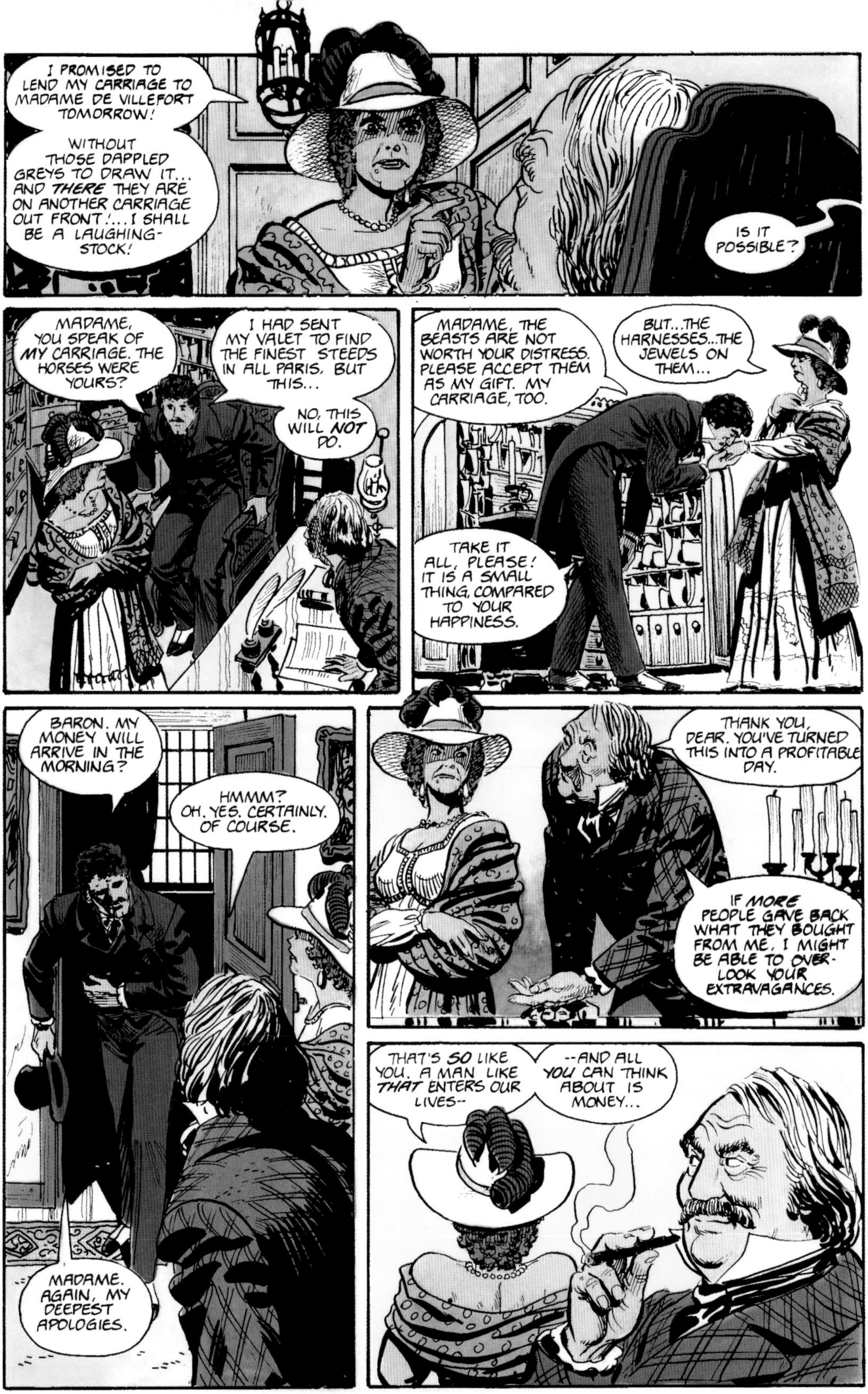

I PROMISED TO LEND MY CARRIAGE TO MADAME DE VILLEFORT TOMORROW!
WITHOUT THOSE DAPPLED GREYS TO DRAW IT... AND THERE THEY ARE ON ANOTHER CARRIAGE OUT FRONT!... I SHALL BE A LAUGHING-STOCK!
IS IT POSSIBLE?
MADAME, YOU SPEAK OF MY CARRIAGE. THE HORSES WERE YOURS?
I HAD SENT MY VALET TO FIND THE FINEST STEEDS IN ALL PARIS, BUT THIS...
NO, THIS WILL NOT DO.
MADAME, THE BEASTS ARE NOT WORTH YOUR DISTRESS. PLEASE ACCEPT THEM AS MY GIFT. MY CARRIAGE, TOO.
BUT... THE HARNESSES... THE JEWELS ON THEM...
TAKE IT ALL, PLEASE! IT IS A SMALL THING, COMPARED TO YOUR HAPPINESS.
BARON. MY MONEY WILL ARRIVE IN THE MORNING?
HMMM? OH. YES. CERTAINLY. OF COURSE.
MADAME. AGAIN, MY DEEPEST APOLOGIES.
THANK YOU, DEAR. YOU'VE TURNED THIS INTO A PROFITABLE DAY.
IF MORE PEOPLE GAVE BACK WHAT THEY BOUGHT FROM ME, I MIGHT BE ABLE TO OVER-LOOK YOUR EXTRAVAGANCES.
THAT'S SO LIKE YOU. A MAN LIKE THAT ENTERS OUR LIVES--
--AND ALL YOU CAN THINK ABOUT IS MONEY...

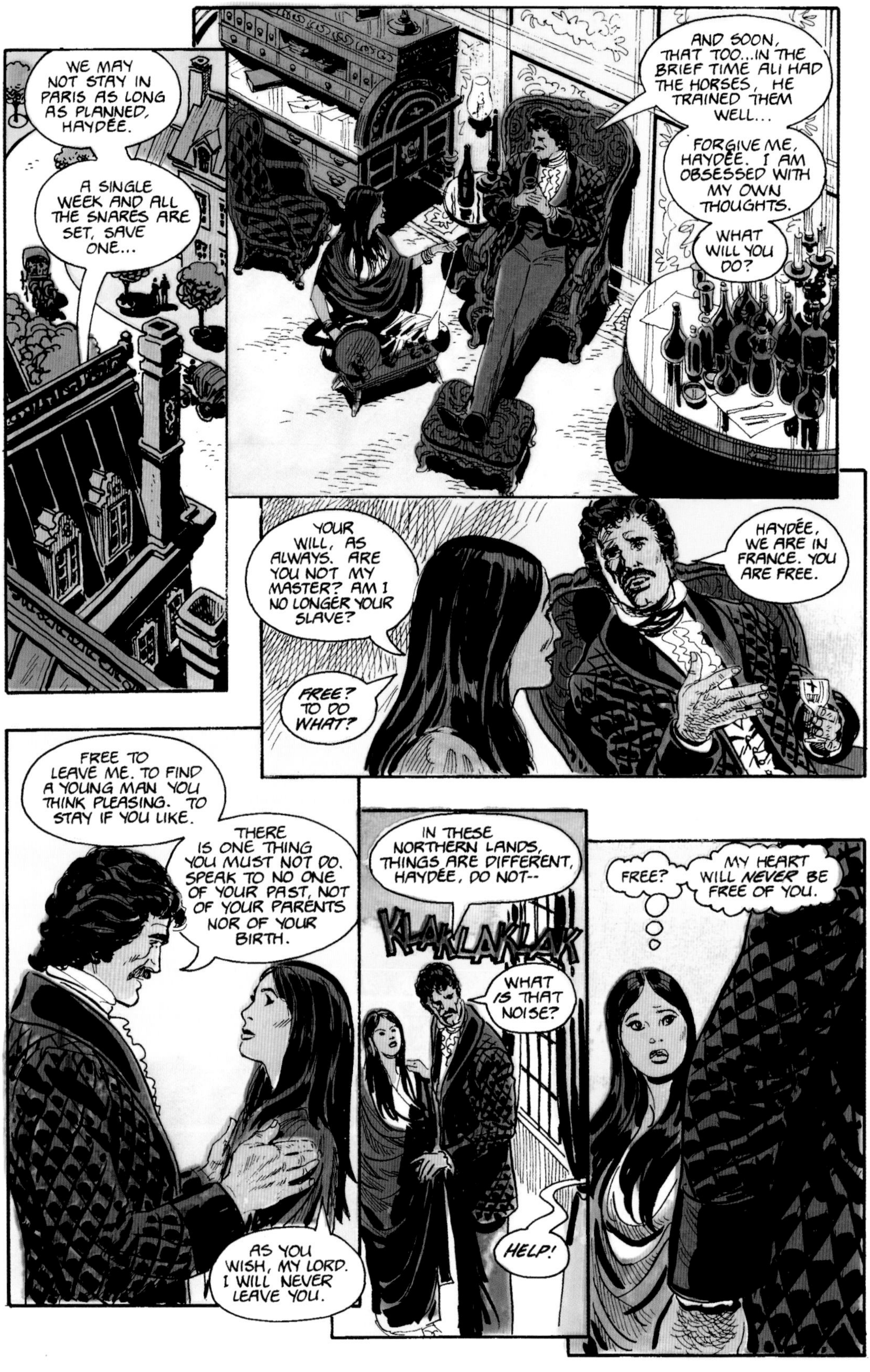
WE MAY NOT STAY IN PARIS AS LONG AS PLANNED, HAYDÉE.
A SINGLE WEEK AND ALL THE SNARES ARE SET, SAVE ONE...
AND SOON, THAT TOO...IN THE BRIEF TIME ALI HAD THE HORSES, HE TRAINED THEM WELL...
FORGIVE ME, HAYDÉE. I AM OBSESSED WITH MY OWN THOUGHTS.
WHAT WILL YOU DO?
YOUR WILL, AS ALWAYS. ARE YOU NOT MY MASTER? AM I NO LONGER YOUR SLAVE?
HAYDÉE, WE ARE IN FRANCE. YOU ARE FREE.
FREE? TO DO WHAT?
FREE TO LEAVE ME. TO FIND A YOUNG MAN YOU THINK PLEASING. TO STAY IF YOU LIKE.
THERE IS ONE THING YOU MUST NOT DO. SPEAK TO NO ONE OF YOUR PAST, NOT OF YOUR PARENTS NOR OF YOUR BIRTH.
AS YOU WISH, MY LORD. I WILL NEVER LEAVE YOU.
IN THESE NORTHERN LANDS, THINGS ARE DIFFERENT, HAYDÉE, DO NOT--
KLAKLAKLAK
WHAT IS THAT NOISE?
HELP!
FREE?
MY HEART WILL NEVER BE FREE OF YOU.

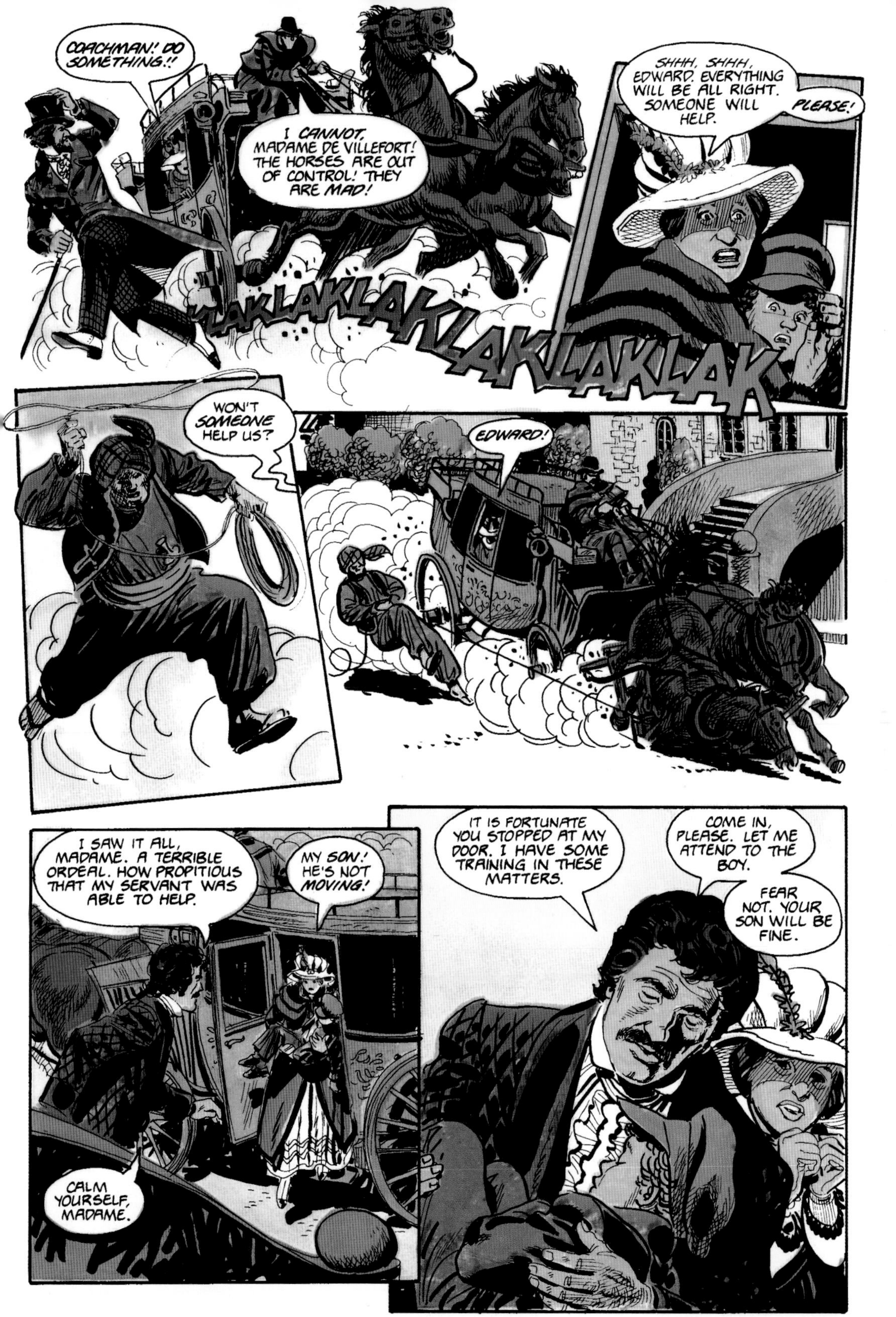
COACHMAN! DO SOMETHING!!
I CANNOT, MADAME DE VILLEFORT! THE HORSES ARE OUT OF CONTROL! THEY ARE MAD!
SHHH, SHHH, EDWARD. EVERYTHING WILL BE ALL RIGHT. SOMEONE WILL HELP.
PLEASE!
KLAKLAKLAKLAKLAK
WON'T SOMEONE HELP US?
EDWARD!
I SAW IT ALL, MADAME. A TERRIBLE ORDEAL. HOW PROPITIOUS THAT MY SERVANT WAS ABLE TO HELP.
MY SON! HE'S NOT MOVING!
CALM YOURSELF, MADAME.
IT IS FORTUNATE YOU STOPPED AT MY DOOR. I HAVE SOME TRAINING IN THESE MATTERS.
COME IN, PLEASE. LET ME ATTEND TO THE BOY.
FEAR NOT. YOUR SON WILL BE FINE.

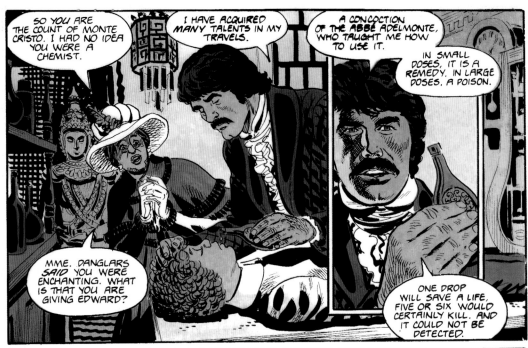

SO YOU ARE THE COUNT OF MONTE CRISTO. I HAD NO IDEA YOU WERE A CHEMIST.

I HAVE ACQUIRED MANY TALENTS IN MY TRAVELS.

A CONCOCTION OF THE ABBÉ ADELMONTE, WHO TAUGHT ME HOW TO USE IT.

IN SMALL DOSES, IT IS A REMEDY. IN LARGE DOSES, A POISON.

MME. DANGLARS *SAID* YOU WERE ENCHANTING. WHAT IS THAT YOU ARE GIVING EDWARD?

ONE DROP WILL SAVE A LIFE, FIVE OR SIX WOULD CERTAINLY KILL. AND IT COULD NOT BE DETECTED.

FORGIVE ME, MADAME. I WILL SAY NO MORE. I DO NOT WISH IT TO SOUND AS THOUGH I WERE ADVISING YOU.

YOUR SON. I PRAY HE WILL NOT SUFFER A RELAPSE.

DO YOU THINK IT LIKELY?

TAKE NO CHANCES-- HERE. IF HE GROWS FAINT, GIVE HIM ANOTHER DROP. BUT ONLY ONE DROP.

I--I CANNOT... YOU HAVE BEEN TOO KIND ALREADY...

I *INSIST.*

WELL...IF... THANK YOU. THANK YOU FOR EVERYTHING.

I SHALL USE THE POTION WISELY.

I *KNOW* YOU WILL, MADAME.

EXCUSE ME FOR BURSTING IN UNINVITED, COUNT, BUT I--

MADAME DE VILLEFORT! I HAD NO IDEA YOU'D BE HERE.

ALBERT.

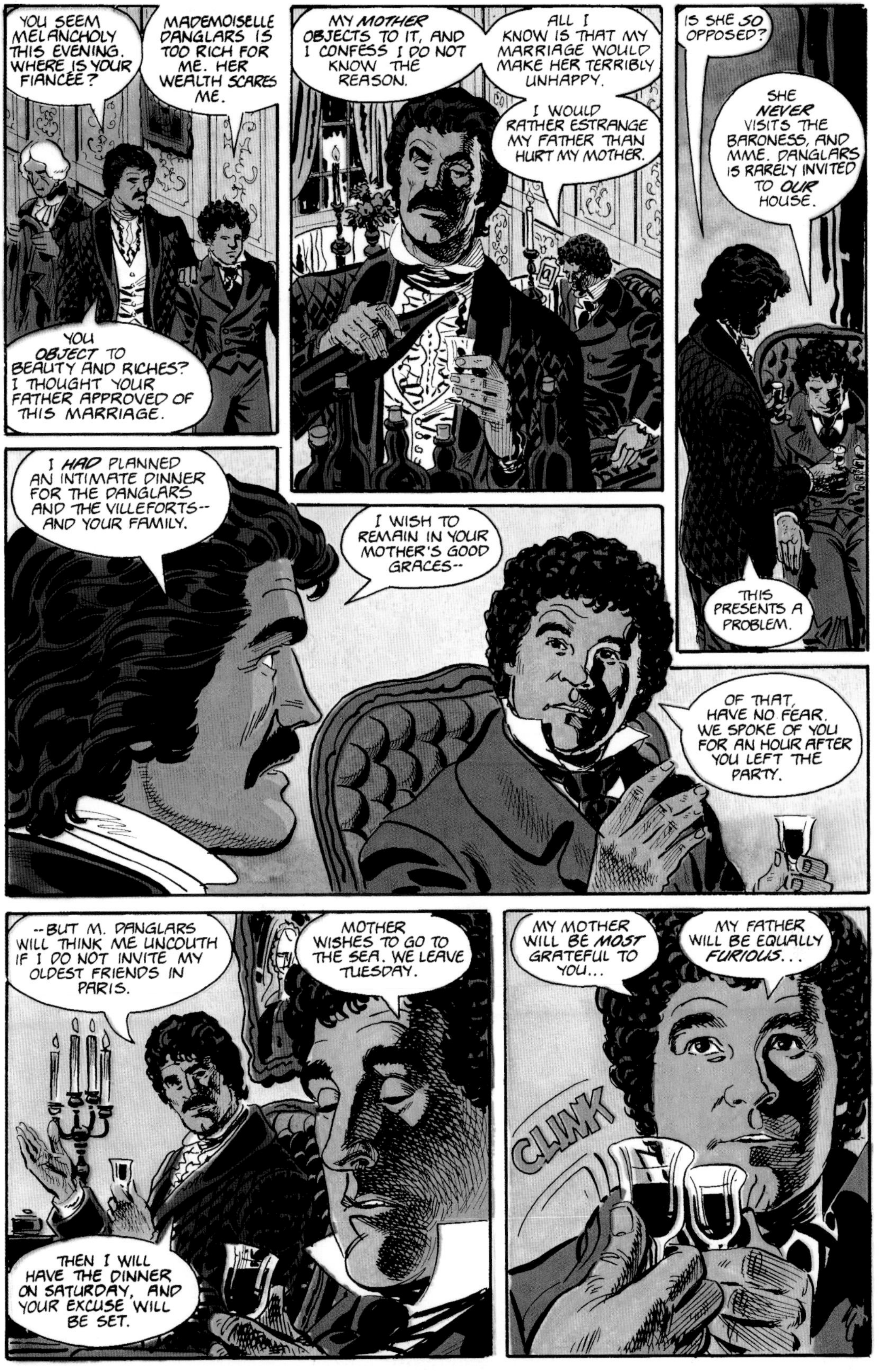
YOU SEEM MELANCHOLY THIS EVENING. WHERE IS YOUR FIANCÉE?
MADEMOISELLE DANGLARS IS TOO RICH FOR ME. HER WEALTH SCARES ME.
YOU *OBJECT* TO BEAUTY AND RICHES? I THOUGHT YOUR FATHER APPROVED OF THIS MARRIAGE.
MY *MOTHER* OBJECTS TO IT, AND I CONFESS I DO NOT KNOW THE REASON.
ALL I KNOW IS THAT MY MARRIAGE WOULD MAKE HER TERRIBLY UNHAPPY.
I WOULD RATHER ESTRANGE MY FATHER THAN HURT MY MOTHER.
IS SHE *SO* OPPOSED?
SHE *NEVER* VISITS THE BARONESS, AND MME. DANGLARS IS RARELY INVITED TO *OUR* HOUSE.
THIS PRESENTS A PROBLEM.
I *HAD* PLANNED AN INTIMATE DINNER FOR THE DANGLARS AND THE VILLEFORTS-- AND YOUR FAMILY.
I WISH TO REMAIN IN YOUR MOTHER'S GOOD GRACES--
OF THAT, HAVE NO FEAR. WE SPOKE OF YOU FOR AN HOUR AFTER YOU LEFT THE PARTY.
--BUT M. DANGLARS WILL THINK ME UNCOUTH IF I DO NOT INVITE MY OLDEST FRIENDS IN PARIS.
MOTHER WISHES TO GO TO THE SEA. WE LEAVE TUESDAY.
THEN I WILL HAVE THE DINNER ON SATURDAY, AND YOUR EXCUSE WILL BE SET.
MY MOTHER WILL BE *MOST* GRATEFUL TO YOU...
MY FATHER WILL BE EQUALLY *FURIOUS*...
CLINK

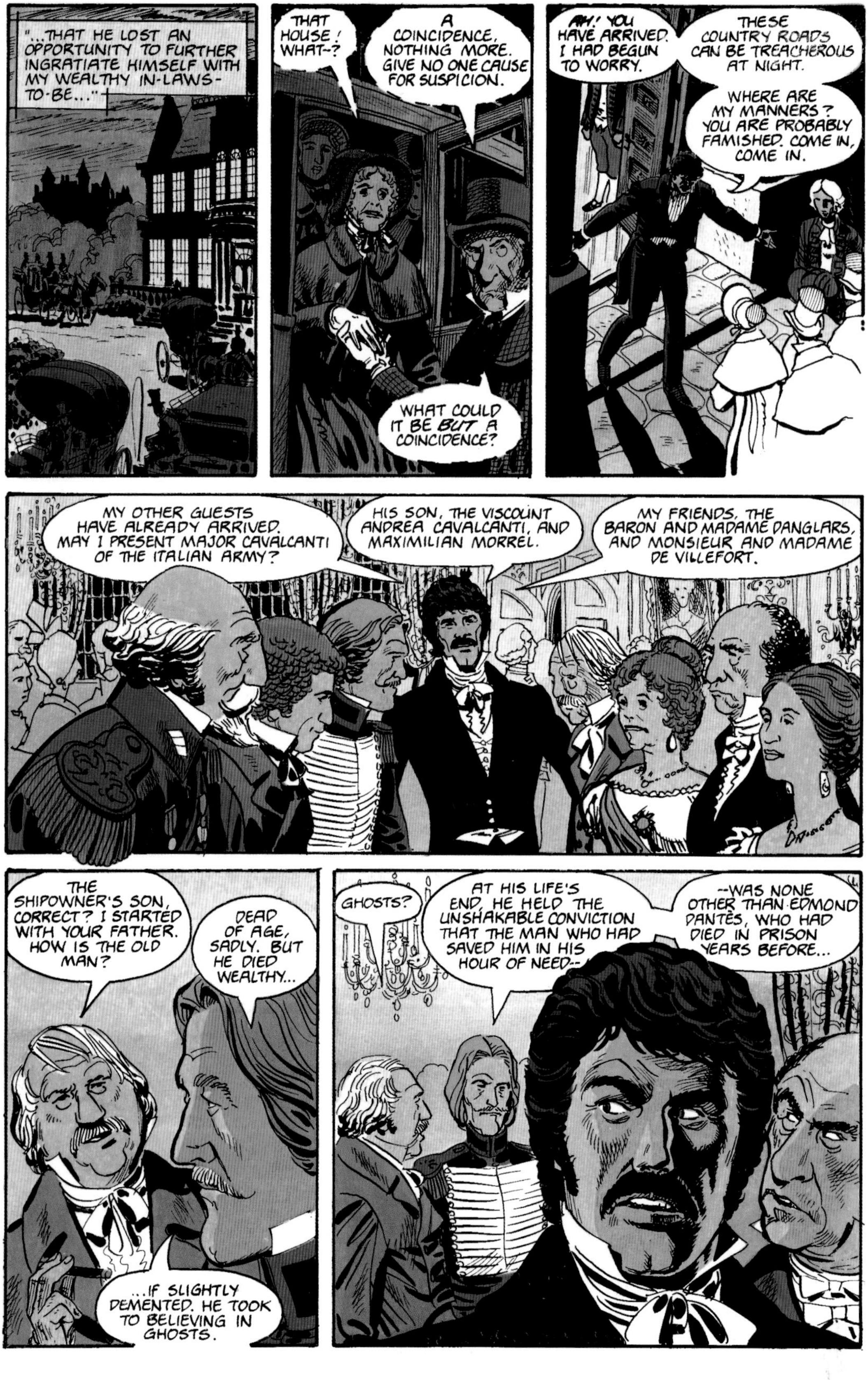
"...THAT HE LOST AN OPPORTUNITY TO FURTHER INGRATIATE HIMSELF WITH MY WEALTHY IN-LAWS-TO-BE..."
THAT HOUSE! WHAT-?
A COINCIDENCE, NOTHING MORE. GIVE NO ONE CAUSE FOR SUSPICION.
WHAT COULD IT BE BUT A COINCIDENCE?
AH! YOU HAVE ARRIVED. I HAD BEGUN TO WORRY.
THESE COUNTRY ROADS CAN BE TREACHEROUS AT NIGHT.
WHERE ARE MY MANNERS? YOU ARE PROBABLY FAMISHED. COME IN, COME IN.
MY OTHER GUESTS HAVE ALREADY ARRIVED. MAY I PRESENT MAJOR CAVALCANTI OF THE ITALIAN ARMY?
HIS SON, THE VISCOUNT ANDREA CAVALCANTI, AND MAXIMILIAN MORREL.
MY FRIENDS, THE BARON AND MADAME DANGLARS, AND MONSIEUR AND MADAME DE VILLEFORT.
THE SHIPOWNER'S SON, CORRECT? I STARTED WITH YOUR FATHER. HOW IS THE OLD MAN?
DEAD OF AGE, SADLY. BUT HE DIED WEALTHY...
...IF SLIGHTLY DEMENTED. HE TOOK TO BELIEVING IN GHOSTS.
GHOSTS?
AT HIS LIFE'S END, HE HELD THE UNSHAKABLE CONVICTION THAT THE MAN WHO HAD SAVED HIM IN HIS HOUR OF NEED--
--WAS NONE OTHER THAN EDMOND DANTÈS, WHO HAD DIED IN PRISON YEARS BEFORE...

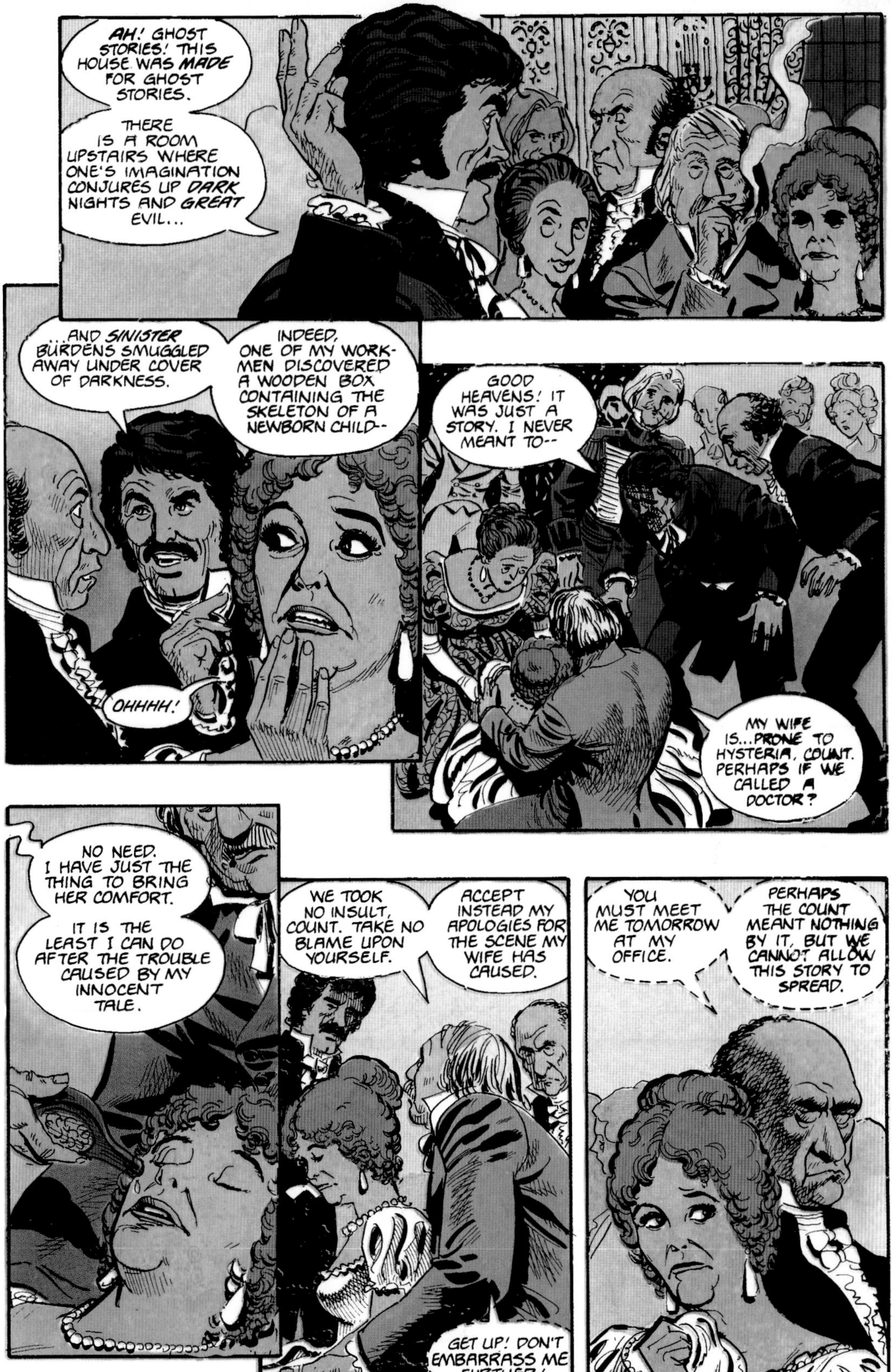
AH! GHOST STORIES! THIS HOUSE WAS MADE FOR GHOST STORIES.
THERE IS A ROOM UPSTAIRS WHERE ONE'S IMAGINATION CONJURES UP DARK NIGHTS AND GREAT EVIL...
...AND SINISTER BURDENS SMUGGLED AWAY UNDER COVER OF DARKNESS.
INDEED, ONE OF MY WORKMEN DISCOVERED A WOODEN BOX CONTAINING THE SKELETON OF A NEWBORN CHILD--
OHHHH!
GOOD HEAVENS! IT WAS JUST A STORY. I NEVER MEANT TO--
MY WIFE IS...PRONE TO HYSTERIA, COUNT. PERHAPS IF WE CALLED A DOCTOR?
NO NEED. I HAVE JUST THE THING TO BRING HER COMFORT.
IT IS THE LEAST I CAN DO AFTER THE TROUBLE CAUSED BY MY INNOCENT TALE.
WE TOOK NO INSULT, COUNT. TAKE NO BLAME UPON YOURSELF.
ACCEPT INSTEAD MY APOLOGIES FOR THE SCENE MY WIFE HAS CAUSED.
GET UP! DON'T EMBARRASS ME FURTHER!
YOU MUST MEET ME TOMORROW AT MY OFFICE.
PERHAPS THE COUNT MEANT NOTHING BY IT, BUT WE CANNOT ALLOW THIS STORY TO SPREAD.

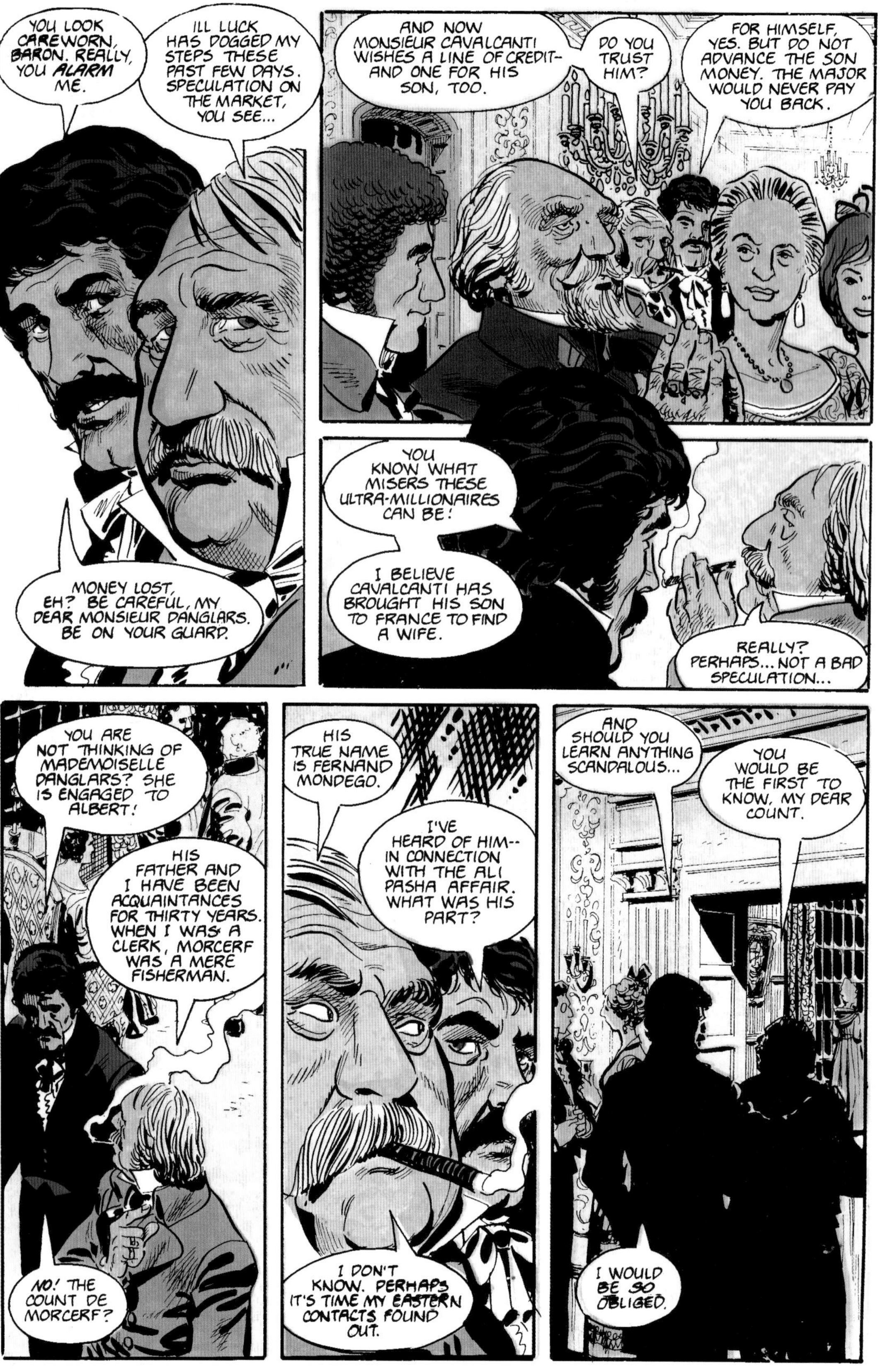
YOU LOOK CAREWORN, BARON. REALLY, YOU ALARM ME.
ILL LUCK HAS DOGGED MY STEPS THESE PAST FEW DAYS. SPECULATION ON THE MARKET, YOU SEE...
MONEY LOST, EH? BE CAREFUL, MY DEAR MONSIEUR DANGLARS. BE ON YOUR GUARD.
AND NOW MONSIEUR CAVALCANTI WISHES A LINE OF CREDIT-- AND ONE FOR HIS SON, TOO.
DO YOU TRUST HIM?
FOR HIMSELF, YES. BUT DO NOT ADVANCE THE SON MONEY. THE MAJOR WOULD NEVER PAY YOU BACK.
YOU KNOW WHAT MISERS THESE ULTRA-MILLIONAIRES CAN BE!
I BELIEVE CAVALCANTI HAS BROUGHT HIS SON TO FRANCE TO FIND A WIFE.
REALLY? PERHAPS... NOT A BAD SPECULATION...
YOU ARE NOT THINKING OF MADEMOISELLE DANGLARS? SHE IS ENGAGED TO ALBERT!
HIS FATHER AND I HAVE BEEN ACQUAINTANCES FOR THIRTY YEARS. WHEN I WAS A CLERK, MORCERF WAS A MERE FISHERMAN.
NO! THE COUNT DE MORCERF?
HIS TRUE NAME IS FERNAND MONDEGO.
I'VE HEARD OF HIM-- IN CONNECTION WITH THE ALI PASHA AFFAIR. WHAT WAS HIS PART?
I DON'T KNOW. PERHAPS IT'S TIME MY EASTERN CONTACTS FOUND OUT.
AND SHOULD YOU LEARN ANYTHING SCANDALOUS...
YOU WOULD BE THE FIRST TO KNOW, MY DEAR COUNT.
I WOULD BE SO OBLIGED.

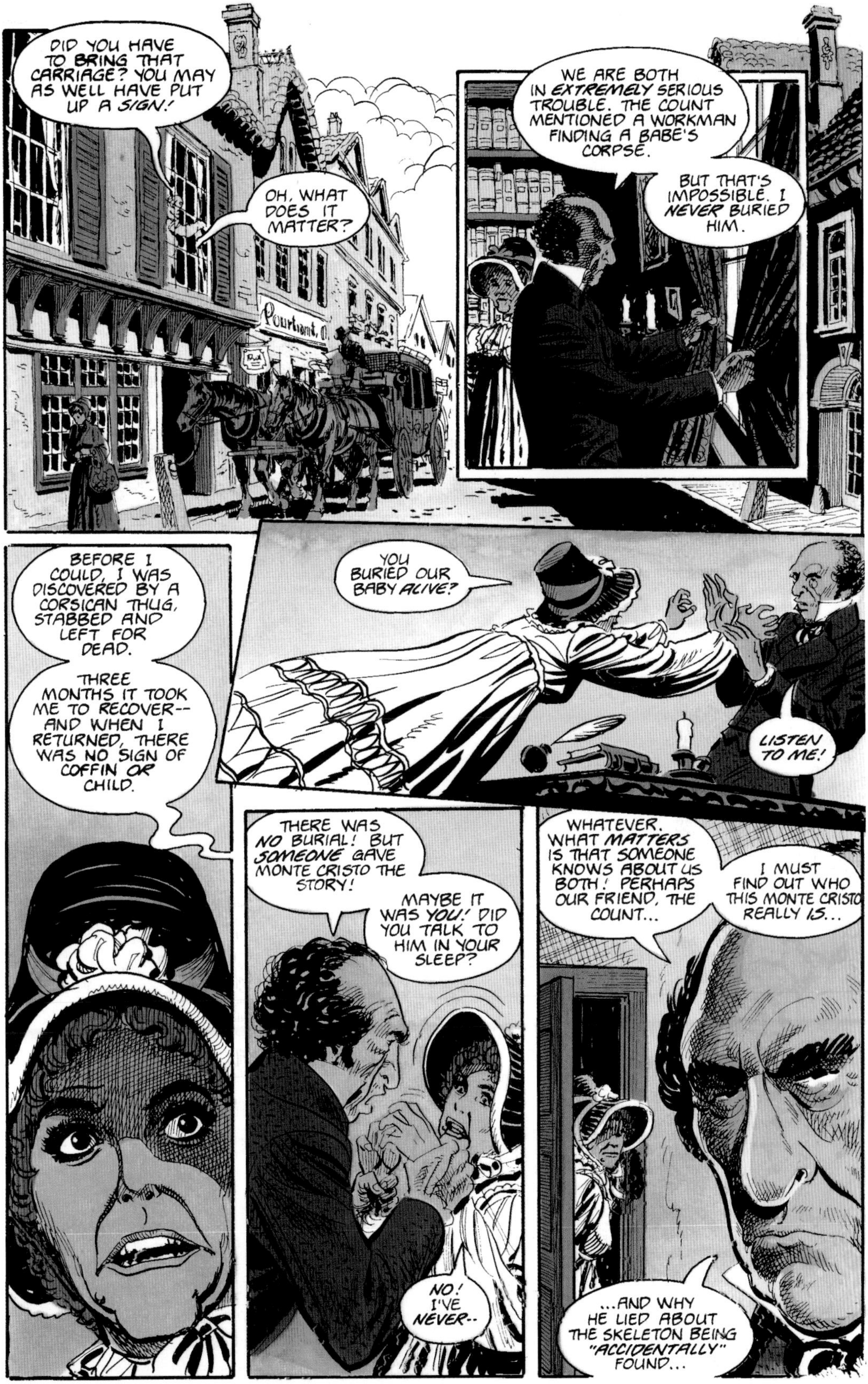
DID YOU HAVE TO BRING THAT CARRIAGE? YOU MAY AS WELL HAVE PUT UP A SIGN!
OH, WHAT DOES IT MATTER?
WE ARE BOTH IN EXTREMELY SERIOUS TROUBLE. THE COUNT MENTIONED A WORKMAN FINDING A BABE'S CORPSE.
BUT THAT'S IMPOSSIBLE. I NEVER BURIED HIM.
BEFORE I COULD, I WAS DISCOVERED BY A CORSICAN THUG, STABBED AND LEFT FOR DEAD.
THREE MONTHS IT TOOK ME TO RECOVER-- AND WHEN I RETURNED, THERE WAS NO SIGN OF COFFIN OR CHILD.
YOU BURIED OUR BABY ALIVE?
LISTEN TO ME!
THERE WAS NO BURIAL! BUT SOMEONE GAVE MONTE CRISTO THE STORY!
MAYBE IT WAS YOU! DID YOU TALK TO HIM IN YOUR SLEEP?
NO! I'VE NEVER--
WHATEVER. WHAT MATTERS IS THAT SOMEONE KNOWS ABOUT US BOTH! PERHAPS OUR FRIEND, THE COUNT...
I MUST FIND OUT WHO THIS MONTE CRISTO REALLY IS...
...AND WHY HE LIED ABOUT THE SKELETON BEING "ACCIDENTALLY" FOUND...

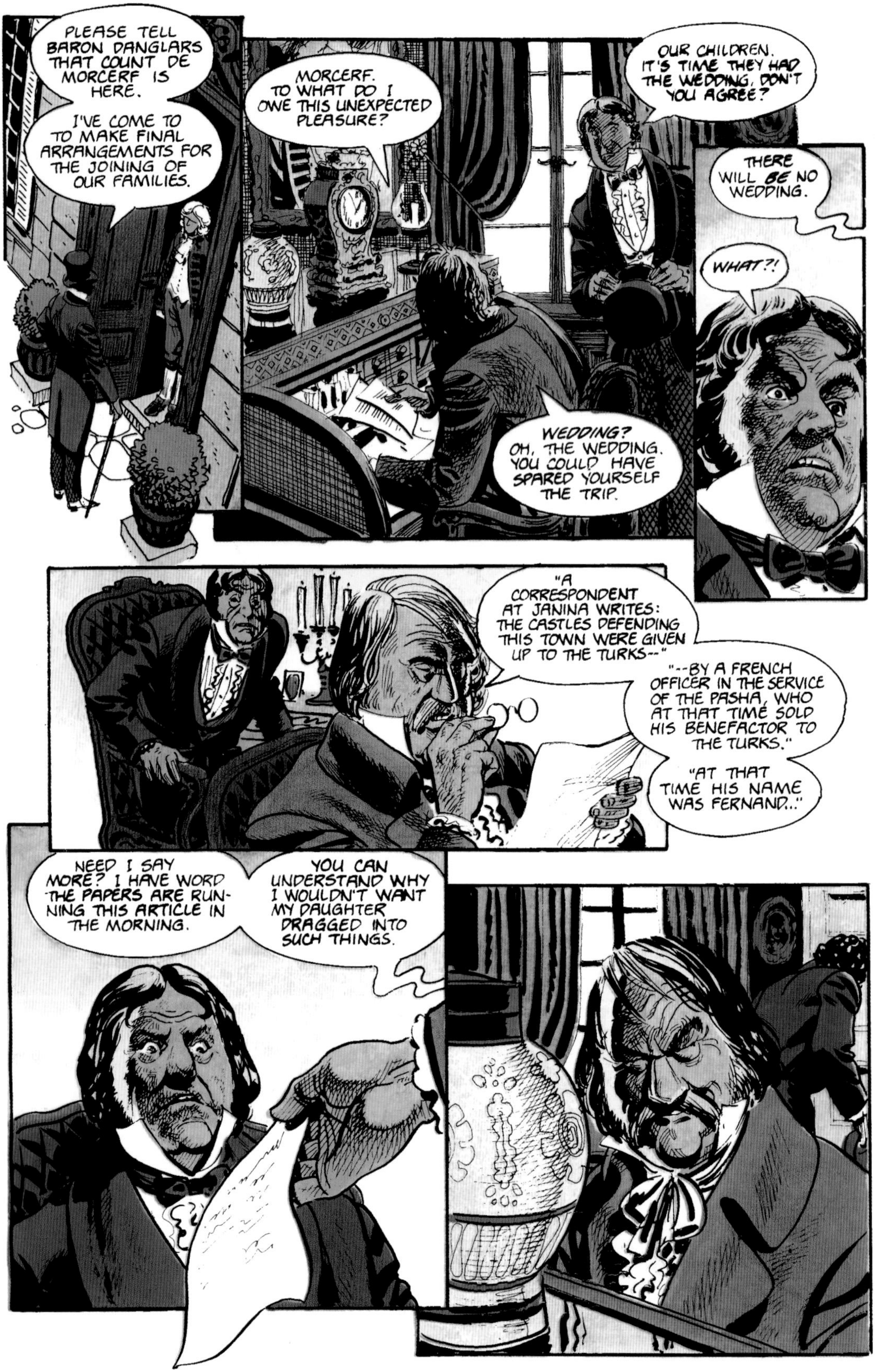
PLEASE TELL BARON DANGLARS THAT COUNT DE MORCERF IS HERE.
I'VE COME TO TO MAKE FINAL ARRANGEMENTS FOR THE JOINING OF OUR FAMILIES.
MORCERF. TO WHAT DO I OWE THIS UNEXPECTED PLEASURE?
OUR CHILDREN. IT'S TIME THEY HAD THE WEDDING, DON'T YOU AGREE?
WEDDING? OH, THE WEDDING. YOU COULD HAVE SPARED YOURSELF THE TRIP.
THERE WILL *BE* NO WEDDING.
WHAT?!
"A CORRESPONDENT AT JANINA WRITES: THE CASTLES DEFENDING THIS TOWN WERE GIVEN UP TO THE TURKS--"
"--BY A FRENCH OFFICER IN THE SERVICE OF THE PASHA, WHO AT THAT TIME SOLD HIS BENEFACTOR TO THE TURKS."
"AT THAT TIME HIS NAME WAS FERNAND..."
NEED I SAY MORE? I HAVE WORD THE PAPERS ARE RUNNING THIS ARTICLE IN THE MORNING.
YOU CAN UNDERSTAND WHY I WOULDN'T WANT MY DAUGHTER DRAGGED INTO SUCH THINGS.

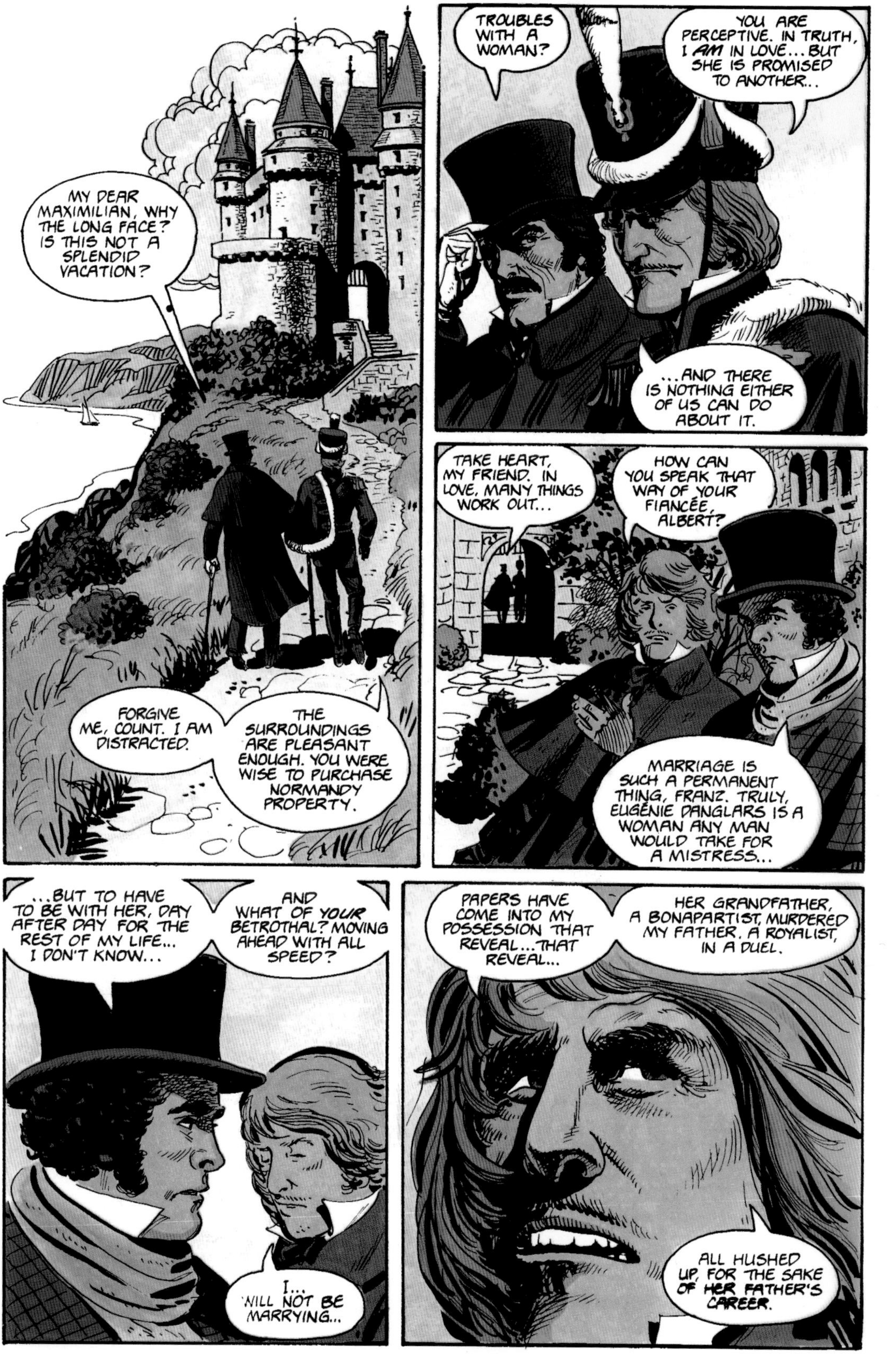
MY DEAR MAXIMILIAN, WHY THE LONG FACE? IS THIS NOT A SPLENDID VACATION?
FORGIVE ME, COUNT. I AM DISTRACTED.
THE SURROUNDINGS ARE PLEASANT ENOUGH. YOU WERE WISE TO PURCHASE NORMANDY PROPERTY.
TROUBLES WITH A WOMAN?
YOU ARE PERCEPTIVE. IN TRUTH, I AM IN LOVE... BUT SHE IS PROMISED TO ANOTHER...
...AND THERE IS NOTHING EITHER OF US CAN DO ABOUT IT.
TAKE HEART, MY FRIEND. IN LOVE, MANY THINGS WORK OUT...
HOW CAN YOU SPEAK THAT WAY OF YOUR FIANCÉE, ALBERT?
MARRIAGE IS SUCH A PERMANENT THING, FRANZ. TRULY, EUGÉNIE DANGLARS IS A WOMAN ANY MAN WOULD TAKE FOR A MISTRESS...
...BUT TO HAVE TO BE WITH HER, DAY AFTER DAY FOR THE REST OF MY LIFE... I DON'T KNOW...
AND WHAT OF YOUR BETROTHAL? MOVING AHEAD WITH ALL SPEED?
I... WILL NOT BE MARRYING...
PAPERS HAVE COME INTO MY POSSESSION THAT REVEAL... THAT REVEAL...
HER GRANDFATHER, A BONAPARTIST, MURDERED MY FATHER, A ROYALIST, IN A DUEL.
ALL HUSHED UP, FOR THE SAKE OF HER FATHER'S CAREER.

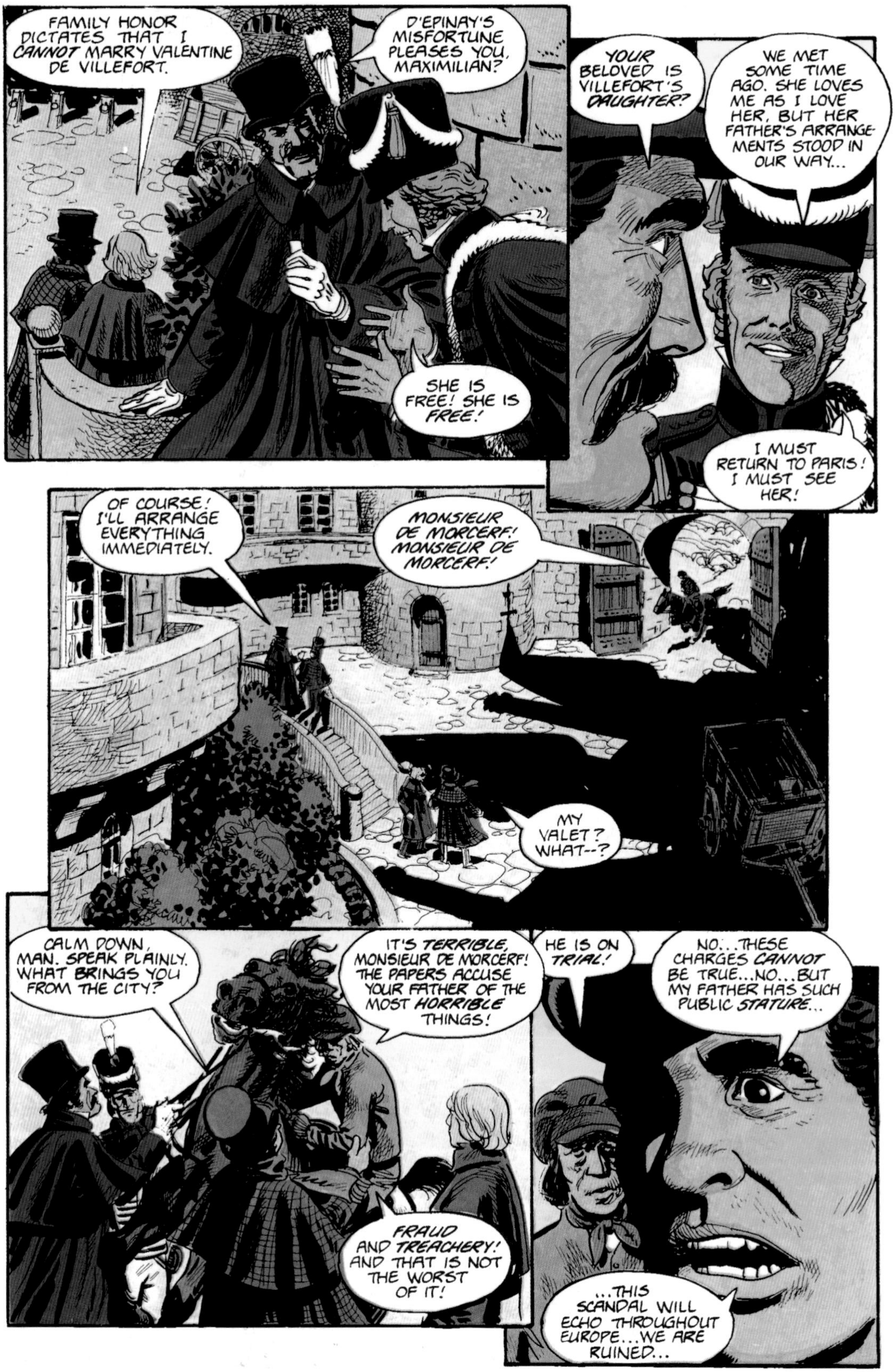
FAMILY HONOR DICTATES THAT I CANNOT MARRY VALENTINE DE VILLEFORT.
D'EPINAY'S MISFORTUNE PLEASES YOU, MAXIMILIAN?
SHE IS FREE! SHE IS FREE!
YOUR BELOVED IS VILLEFORT'S DAUGHTER?
WE MET SOME TIME AGO. SHE LOVES ME AS I LOVE HER, BUT HER FATHER'S ARRANGE-MENTS STOOD IN OUR WAY...
I MUST RETURN TO PARIS! I MUST SEE HER!
OF COURSE! I'LL ARRANGE EVERYTHING IMMEDIATELY.
MONSIEUR DE MORCERF! MONSIEUR DE MORCERF!
MY VALET? WHAT--?
CALM DOWN, MAN. SPEAK PLAINLY. WHAT BRINGS YOU FROM THE CITY?
IT'S TERRIBLE, MONSIEUR DE MORCERF! THE PAPERS ACCUSE YOUR FATHER OF THE MOST HORRIBLE THINGS!
FRAUD AND TREACHERY! AND THAT IS NOT THE WORST OF IT!
HE IS ON TRIAL!
NO...THESE CHARGES CANNOT BE TRUE...NO...BUT MY FATHER HAS SUCH PUBLIC STATURE...
...THIS SCANDAL WILL ECHO THROUGHOUT EUROPE...WE ARE RUINED...

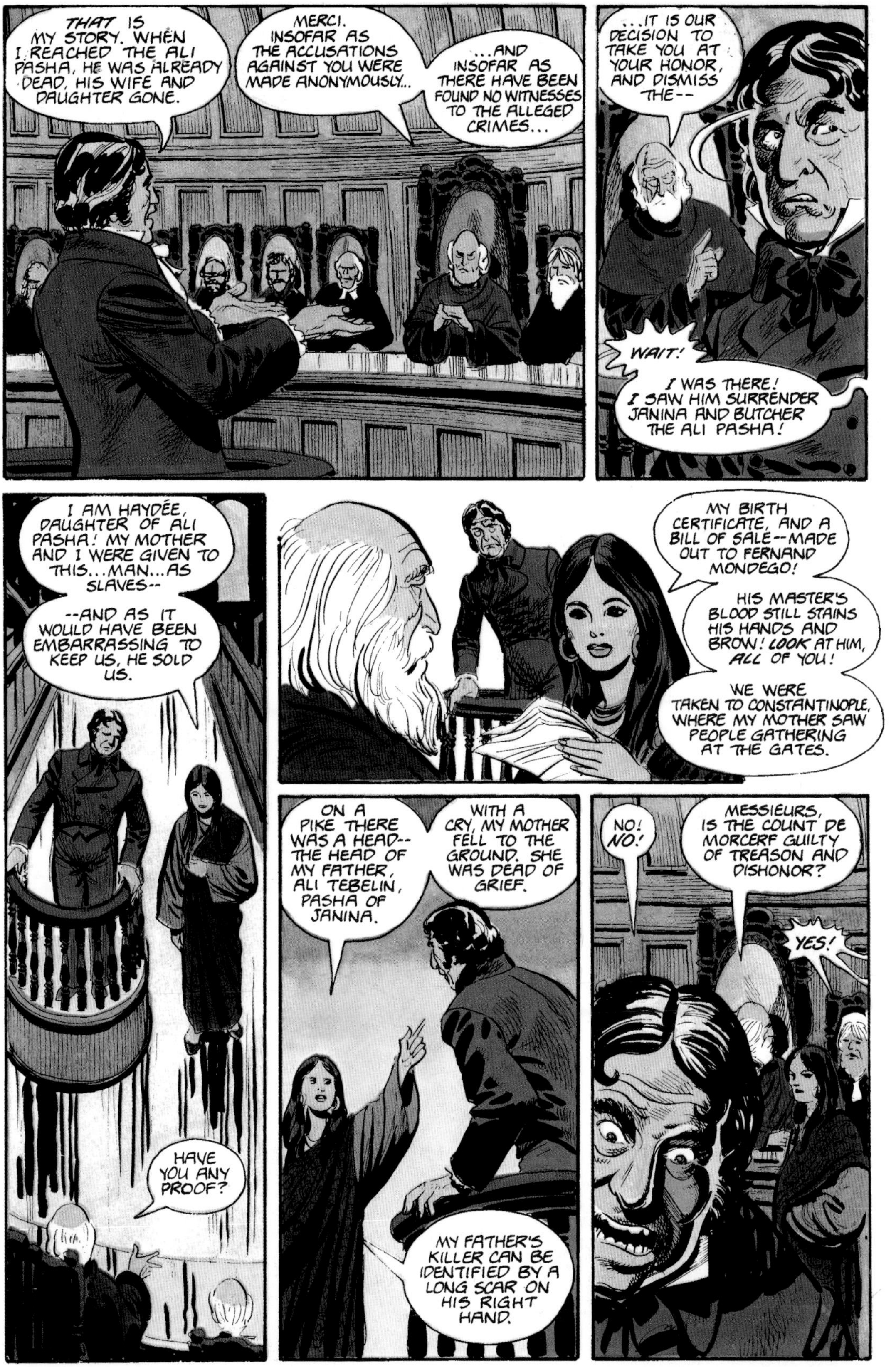
THAT IS MY STORY. WHEN I REACHED THE ALI PASHA, HE WAS ALREADY DEAD, HIS WIFE AND DAUGHTER GONE.
MERCI. INSOFAR AS THE ACCUSATIONS AGAINST YOU WERE MADE ANONYMOUSLY...
...AND INSOFAR AS THERE HAVE BEEN FOUND NO WITNESSES TO THE ALLEGED CRIMES...
...IT IS OUR DECISION TO TAKE YOU AT YOUR HONOR, AND DISMISS THE--
WAIT!
I WAS THERE! I SAW HIM SURRENDER JANINA AND BUTCHER THE ALI PASHA!
I AM HAYDÉE, DAUGHTER OF ALI PASHA! MY MOTHER AND I WERE GIVEN TO THIS...MAN...AS SLAVES--
--AND AS IT WOULD HAVE BEEN EMBARRASSING TO KEEP US, HE SOLD US.
HAVE YOU ANY PROOF?
MY BIRTH CERTIFICATE, AND A BILL OF SALE--MADE OUT TO FERNAND MONDEGO!
HIS MASTER'S BLOOD STILL STAINS HIS HANDS AND BROW! LOOK AT HIM, ALL OF YOU!
WE WERE TAKEN TO CONSTANTINOPLE, WHERE MY MOTHER SAW PEOPLE GATHERING AT THE GATES.
ON A PIKE THERE WAS A HEAD-- THE HEAD OF MY FATHER, ALI TEBELIN, PASHA OF JANINA.
WITH A CRY, MY MOTHER FELL TO THE GROUND. SHE WAS DEAD OF GRIEF.
MY FATHER'S KILLER CAN BE IDENTIFIED BY A LONG SCAR ON HIS RIGHT HAND.
NO! NO!
MESSIEURS, IS THE COUNT DE MORCERF GUILTY OF TREASON AND DISHONOR?
YES!

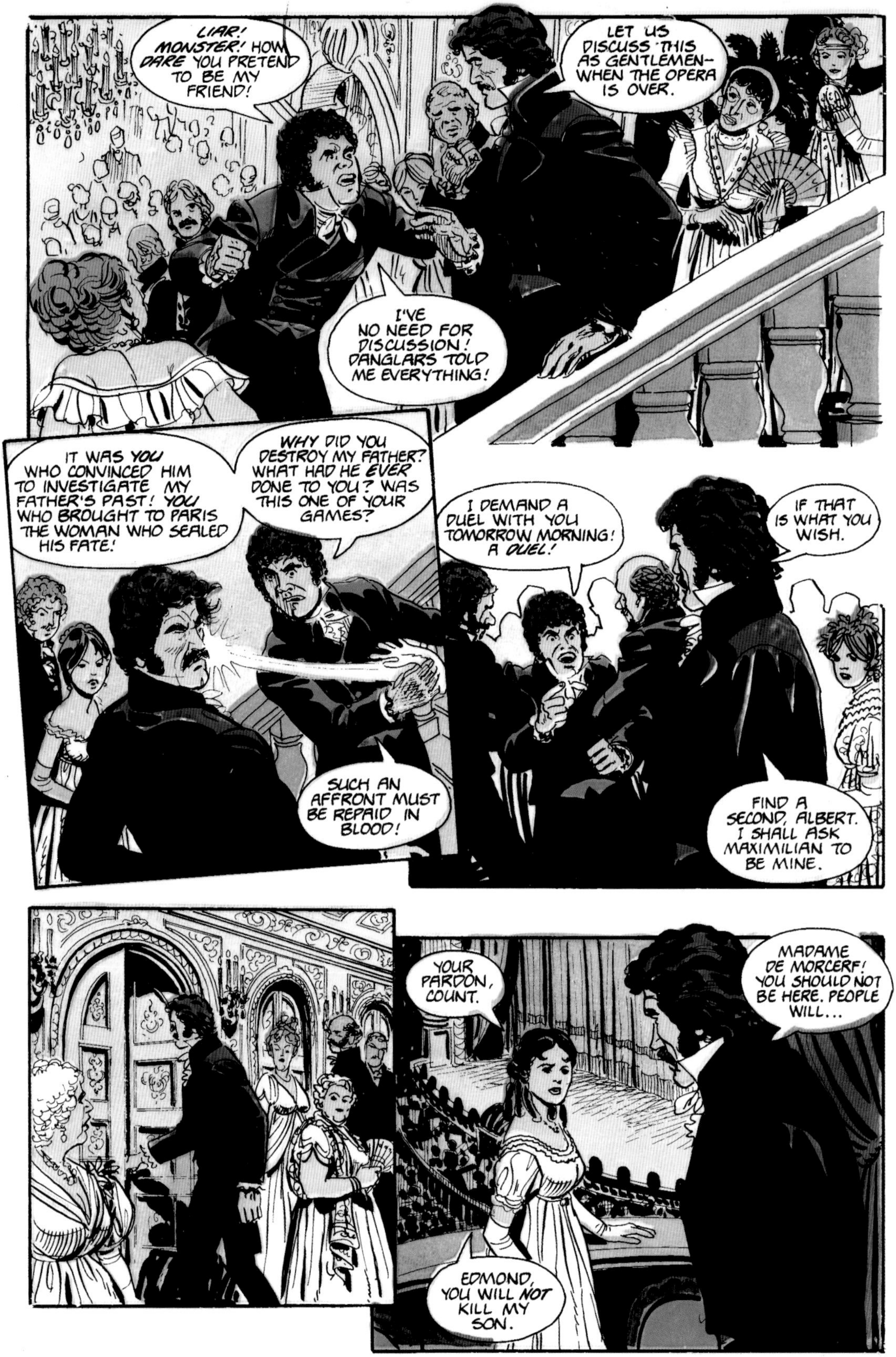
LIAR! MONSTER! HOW DARE YOU PRETEND TO BE MY FRIEND!
LET US DISCUSS THIS AS GENTLEMEN-- WHEN THE OPERA IS OVER.
I'VE NO NEED FOR DISCUSSION! DANGLARS TOLD ME EVERYTHING!
IT WAS YOU WHO CONVINCED HIM TO INVESTIGATE MY FATHER'S PAST! YOU WHO BROUGHT TO PARIS THE WOMAN WHO SEALED HIS FATE!
WHY DID YOU DESTROY MY FATHER? WHAT HAD HE EVER DONE TO YOU? WAS THIS ONE OF YOUR GAMES?
SUCH AN AFFRONT MUST BE REPAID IN BLOOD!
I DEMAND A DUEL WITH YOU TOMORROW MORNING! A DUEL!
IF THAT IS WHAT YOU WISH.
FIND A SECOND, ALBERT. I SHALL ASK MAXIMILIAN TO BE MINE.
YOUR PARDON, COUNT.
MADAME DE MORCERF! YOU SHOULD NOT BE HERE. PEOPLE WILL...
EDMOND, YOU WILL NOT KILL MY SON.

WHAT DID YOU CALL ME, MADAME DE MORCERF?

YOUR *NAME!* IT IS NOT MADAME DE MORCERF WHO PLEADS WITH YOU. IT IS MERCÉDÈS.

MERCÉDÈS IS DEAD.

NO. SHE *LIVES.* SHE REMEMBERS. SHE KNOWS WHO STRUCK DOWN MONSIEUR DE MORCERF.

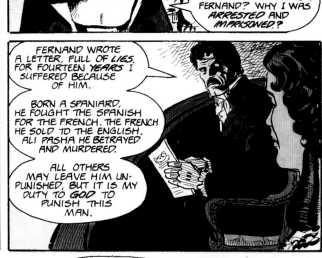

AS NAMES OBSESS YOU, MADAME, CALL HIM FERNAND.

DO YOU *KNOW* WHY YOU WERE LEFT ALONE FOR FERNAND? WHY I WAS *ARRESTED* AND *IMPRISONED*?

FERNAND WROTE A LETTER, FULL OF LIES. FOR FOURTEEN *YEARS* I SUFFERED BECAUSE OF HIM.

BORN A SPANIARD, HE FOUGHT THE SPANISH FOR THE FRENCH. THE FRENCH HE SOLD TO THE ENGLISH. ALI PASHA HE BETRAYED AND MURDERED.

ALL OTHERS MAY LEAVE HIM UN-PUNISHED, BUT IT IS MY DUTY TO *GOD* TO PUNISH THIS MAN.

PUNISH HIM THEN. PUNISH *ME.* BUT DO NOT HURT MY SON.

I WAS PUBLICLY INSULTED, MADAME. I *MUST* DUEL HIM.

EDMOND...

VERY WELL. IT WILL TAKE PLACE-- BUT *MY* BLOOD, NOT ALBERT'S, WILL STAIN THE GROUND.

WOULD THERE WERE ANOTHER WAY, BUT...AH, YOU ARE STILL THE FINE AND NOBLE MAN I LOVE.

I LEARNED SOMETHING OF SUFFERING, TOO, EDMOND, WHEN I LOST YOU.

FAREWELL, EDMOND. FAREWELL. AND THANK YOU.

CURSE THIS VENGEANCE.

CURSE ME.

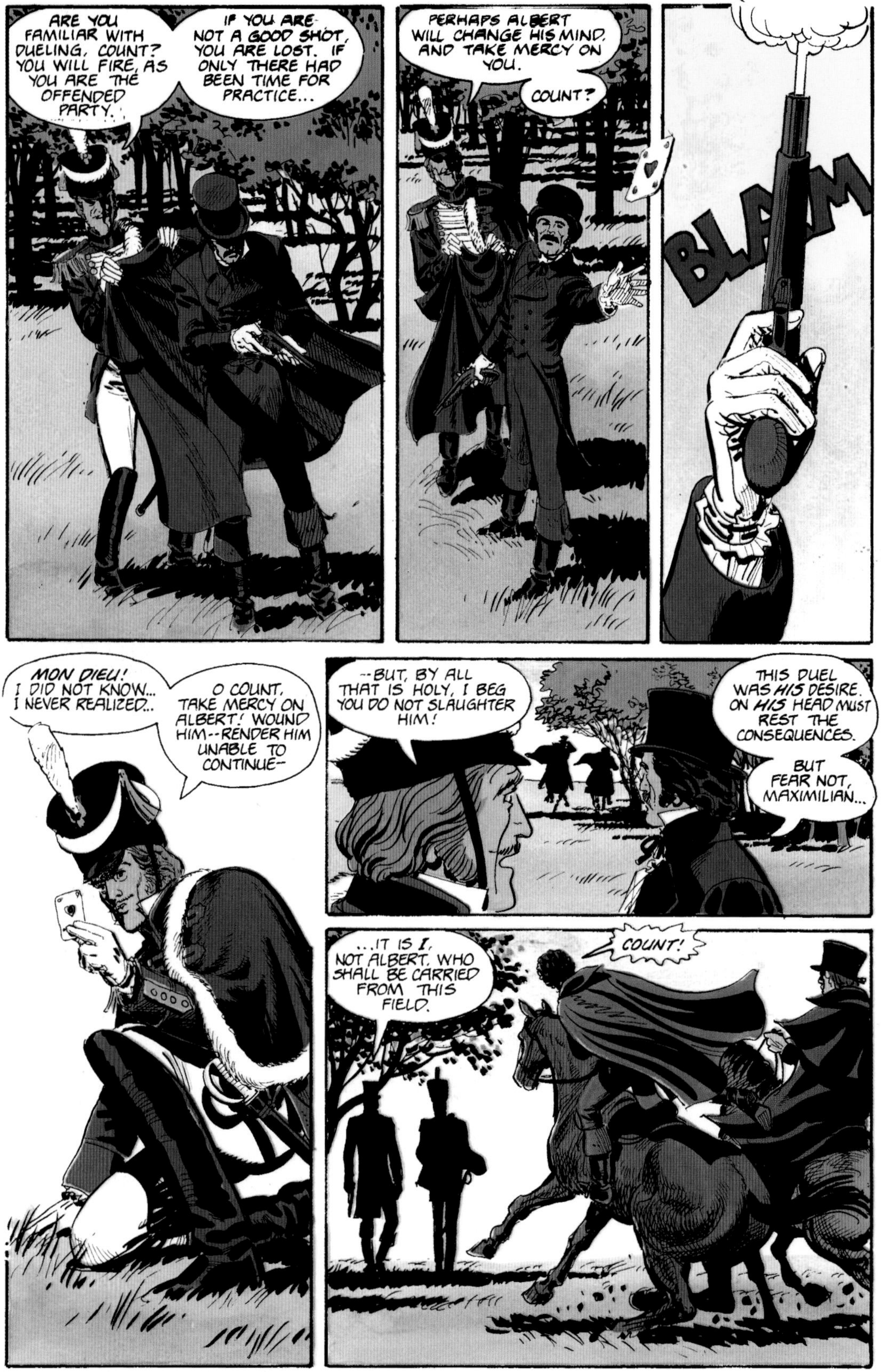

ARE YOU FAMILIAR WITH DUELING, COUNT? YOU WILL FIRE, AS YOU ARE THE OFFENDED PARTY.
IF YOU ARE NOT A GOOD SHOT, YOU ARE LOST. IF ONLY THERE HAD BEEN TIME FOR PRACTICE...
PERHAPS ALBERT WILL CHANGE HIS MIND, AND TAKE MERCY ON YOU.
COUNT?
BLAM
MON DIEU! I DID NOT KNOW... I NEVER REALIZED...
O COUNT, TAKE MERCY ON ALBERT! WOUND HIM--RENDER HIM UNABLE TO CONTINUE--
--BUT, BY ALL THAT IS HOLY, I BEG YOU DO NOT SLAUGHTER HIM!
THIS DUEL WAS HIS DESIRE. ON HIS HEAD MUST REST THE CONSEQUENCES.
BUT FEAR NOT, MAXIMILIAN...
...IT IS I, NOT ALBERT, WHO SHALL BE CARRIED FROM THIS FIELD.
COUNT!

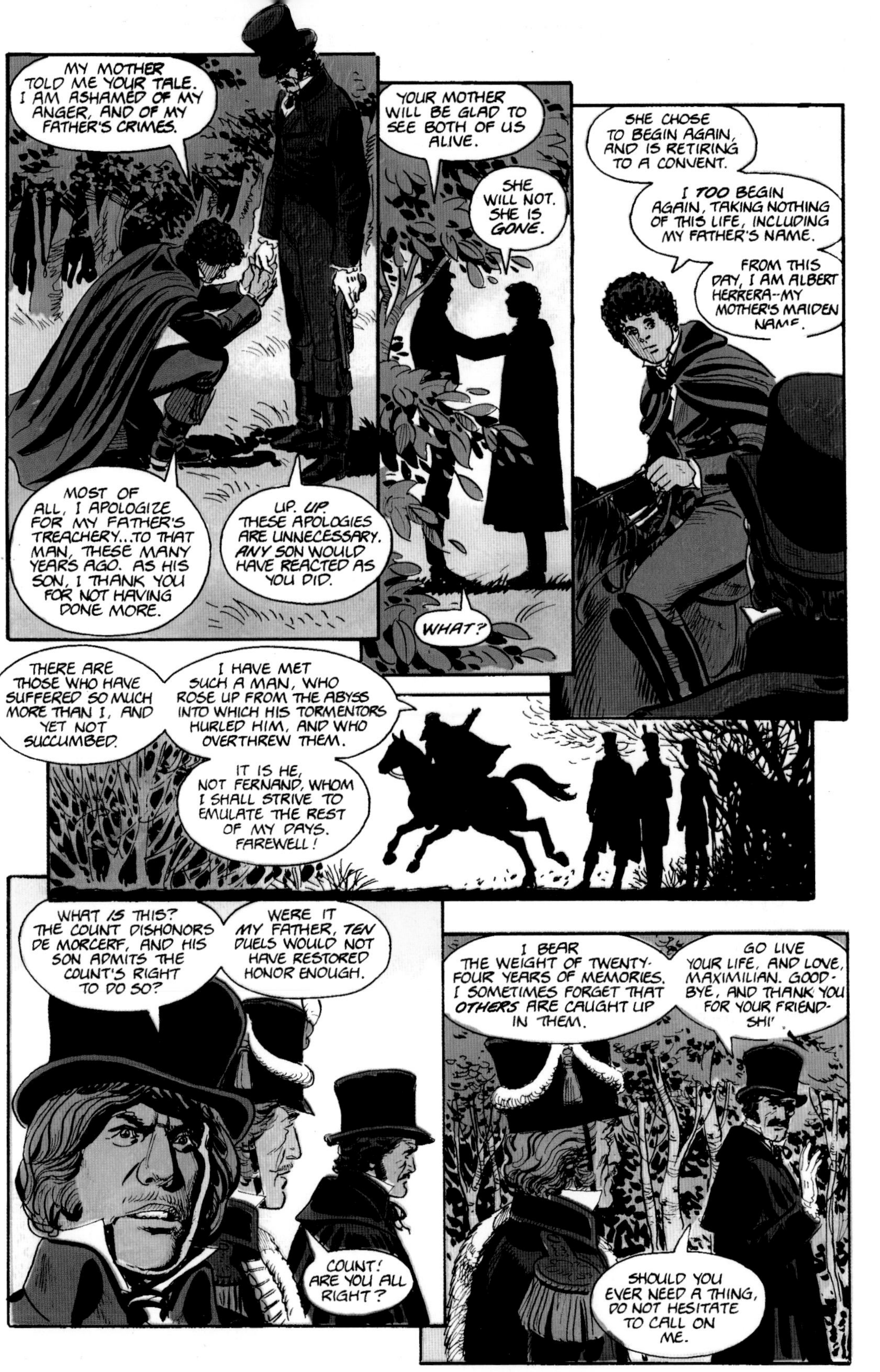
MY MOTHER TOLD ME YOUR TALE. I AM ASHAMED OF MY ANGER, AND OF MY FATHER'S CRIMES.
MOST OF ALL, I APOLOGIZE FOR MY FATHER'S TREACHERY...TO THAT MAN, THESE MANY YEARS AGO. AS HIS SON, I THANK YOU FOR NOT HAVING DONE MORE.
UP. UP. THESE APOLOGIES ARE UNNECESSARY. ANY SON WOULD HAVE REACTED AS YOU DID.
YOUR MOTHER WILL BE GLAD TO SEE BOTH OF US ALIVE.
SHE WILL NOT. SHE IS GONE.
WHAT?
SHE CHOSE TO BEGIN AGAIN, AND IS RETIRING TO A CONVENT.
I TOO BEGIN AGAIN, TAKING NOTHING OF THIS LIFE, INCLUDING MY FATHER'S NAME.
FROM THIS DAY, I AM ALBERT HERRERA--MY MOTHER'S MAIDEN NAME.
THERE ARE THOSE WHO HAVE SUFFERED SO MUCH MORE THAN I, AND YET NOT SUCCUMBED.
I HAVE MET SUCH A MAN, WHO ROSE UP FROM THE ABYSS INTO WHICH HIS TORMENTORS HURLED HIM, AND WHO OVERTHREW THEM.
IT IS HE, NOT FERNAND, WHOM I SHALL STRIVE TO EMULATE THE REST OF MY DAYS. FAREWELL!
WHAT IS THIS? THE COUNT DISHONORS DE MORCERF, AND HIS SON ADMITS THE COUNT'S RIGHT TO DO SO?
WERE IT MY FATHER, TEN DUELS WOULD NOT HAVE RESTORED HONOR ENOUGH.
COUNT! ARE YOU ALL RIGHT?
I BEAR THE WEIGHT OF TWENTY-FOUR YEARS OF MEMORIES. I SOMETIMES FORGET THAT OTHERS ARE CAUGHT UP IN THEM.
GO LIVE YOUR LIFE, AND LOVE, MAXIMILIAN. GOOD-BYE, AND THANK YOU FOR YOUR FRIEND-SHI'
SHOULD YOU EVER NEED A THING, DO NOT HESITATE TO CALL ON ME.

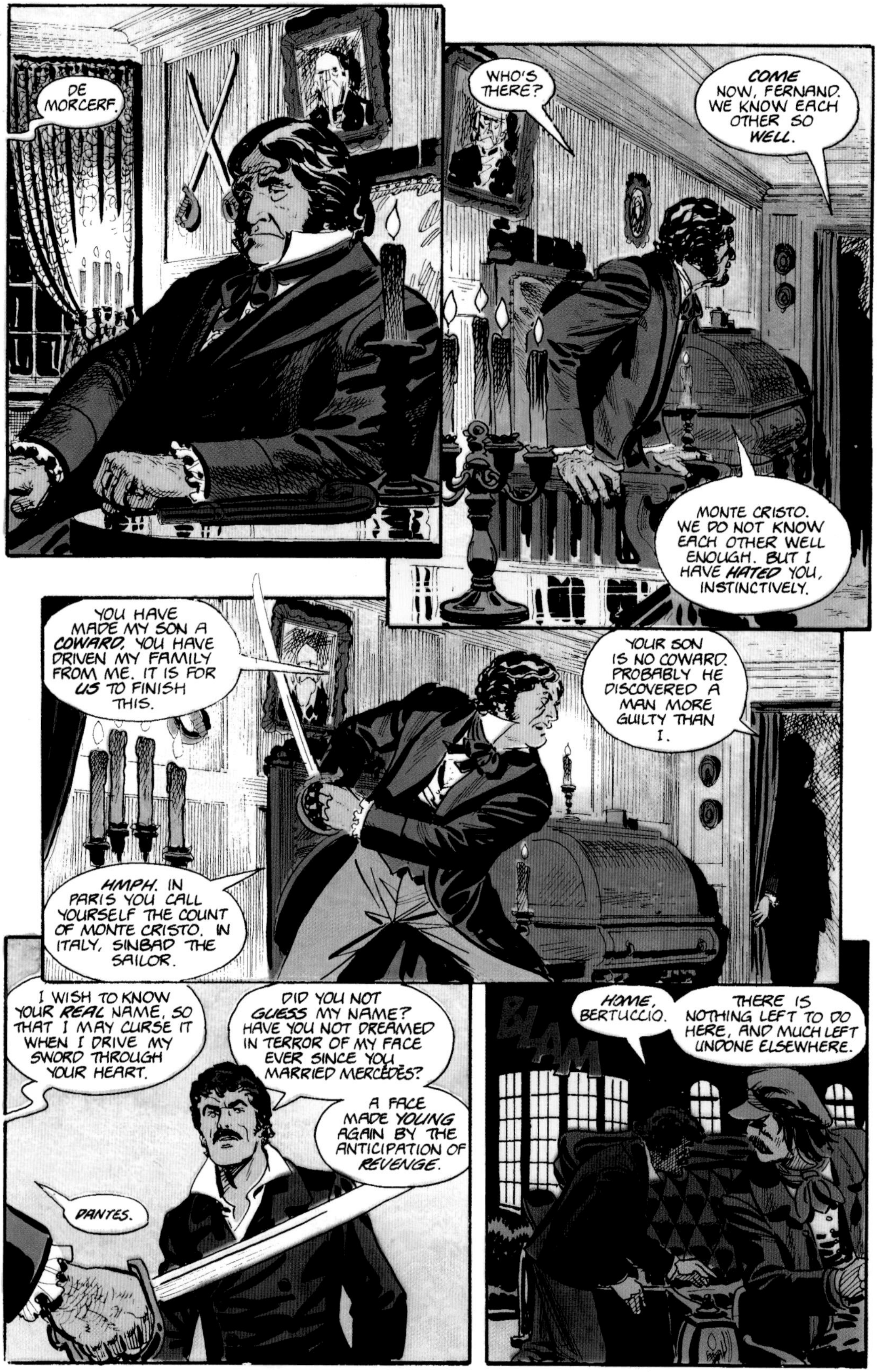
DE MORCERF.
WHO'S THERE?
COME NOW, FERNAND. WE KNOW EACH OTHER SO WELL.
MONTE CRISTO. WE DO NOT KNOW EACH OTHER WELL ENOUGH. BUT I HAVE HATED YOU, INSTINCTIVELY.
YOU HAVE MADE MY SON A COWARD, YOU HAVE DRIVEN MY FAMILY FROM ME. IT IS FOR US TO FINISH THIS.
YOUR SON IS NO COWARD. PROBABLY HE DISCOVERED A MAN MORE GUILTY THAN I.
HMPH. IN PARIS YOU CALL YOURSELF THE COUNT OF MONTE CRISTO. IN ITALY, SINBAD THE SAILOR.
I WISH TO KNOW YOUR REAL NAME, SO THAT I MAY CURSE IT WHEN I DRIVE MY SWORD THROUGH YOUR HEART.
DID YOU NOT GUESS MY NAME? HAVE YOU NOT DREAMED IN TERROR OF MY FACE EVER SINCE YOU MARRIED MERCÉDÈS?
A FACE MADE YOUNG AGAIN BY THE ANTICIPATION OF REVENGE.
DANTES.
BLAM
HOME, BERTUCCIO.
THERE IS NOTHING LEFT TO DO HERE, AND MUCH LEFT UNDONE ELSEWHERE.

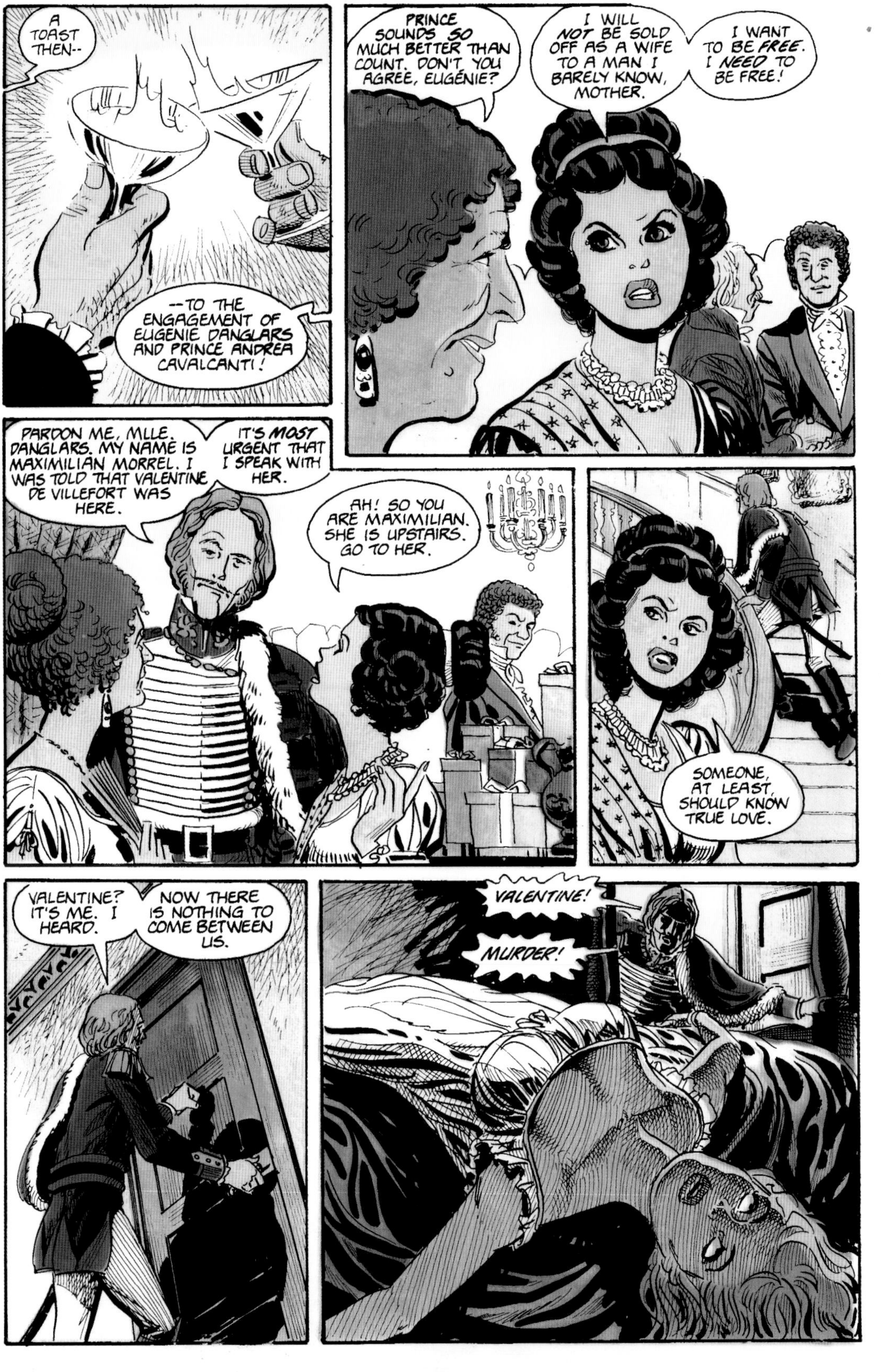

A TOAST THEN--
--TO THE ENGAGEMENT OF EUGENIE DANGLARS AND PRINCE ANDREA CAVALCANTI!
PRINCE SOUNDS SO MUCH BETTER THAN COUNT. DON'T YOU AGREE, EUGÉNIE?
I WILL NOT BE SOLD OFF AS A WIFE TO A MAN I BARELY KNOW, MOTHER.
I WANT TO BE FREE. I NEED TO BE FREE!
PARDON ME, MLLE. DANGLARS. MY NAME IS MAXIMILIAN MORREL. I WAS TOLD THAT VALENTINE DE VILLEFORT WAS HERE.
IT'S MOST URGENT THAT I SPEAK WITH HER.
AH! SO YOU ARE MAXIMILIAN. SHE IS UPSTAIRS. GO TO HER.
SOMEONE, AT LEAST, SHOULD KNOW TRUE LOVE.
VALENTINE? IT'S ME. I HEARD.
NOW THERE IS NOTHING TO COME BETWEEN US.
VALENTINE!
MURDER!

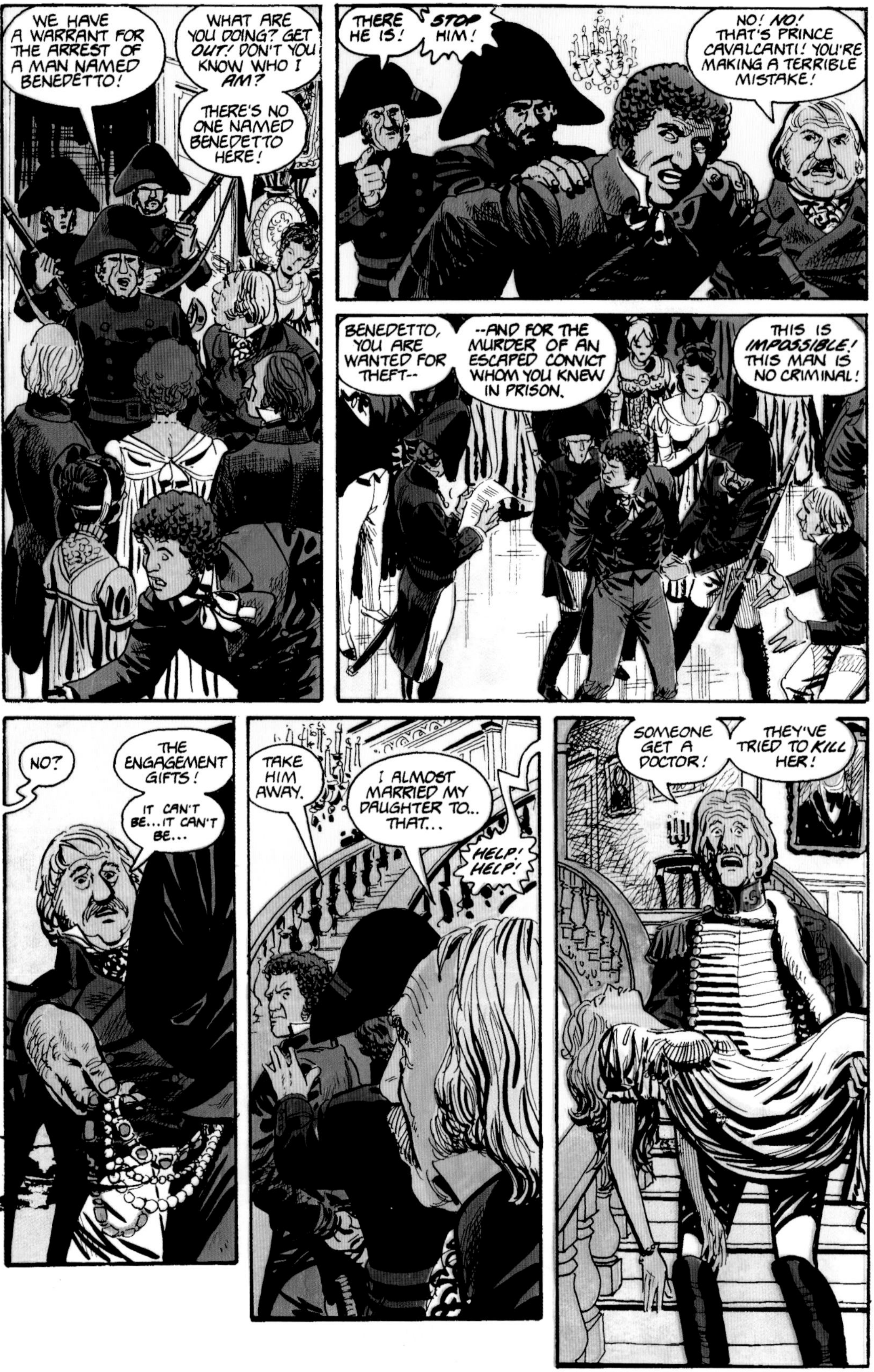
WE HAVE A WARRANT FOR THE ARREST OF A MAN NAMED BENEDETTO!
WHAT ARE YOU DOING? GET OUT! DON'T YOU KNOW WHO I AM?
THERE'S NO ONE NAMED BENEDETTO HERE!
THERE HE IS!
STOP HIM!
NO! NO! THAT'S PRINCE CAVALCANTI! YOU'RE MAKING A TERRIBLE MISTAKE!
BENEDETTO, YOU ARE WANTED FOR THEFT--
--AND FOR THE MURDER OF AN ESCAPED CONVICT WHOM YOU KNEW IN PRISON.
THIS IS IMPOSSIBLE! THIS MAN IS NO CRIMINAL!
NO?
THE ENGAGEMENT GIFTS!
IT CAN'T BE...IT CAN'T BE...
TAKE HIM AWAY.
I ALMOST MARRIED MY DAUGHTER TO... THAT...
HELP! HELP!
SOMEONE GET A DOCTOR!
THEY'VE TRIED TO KILL HER!

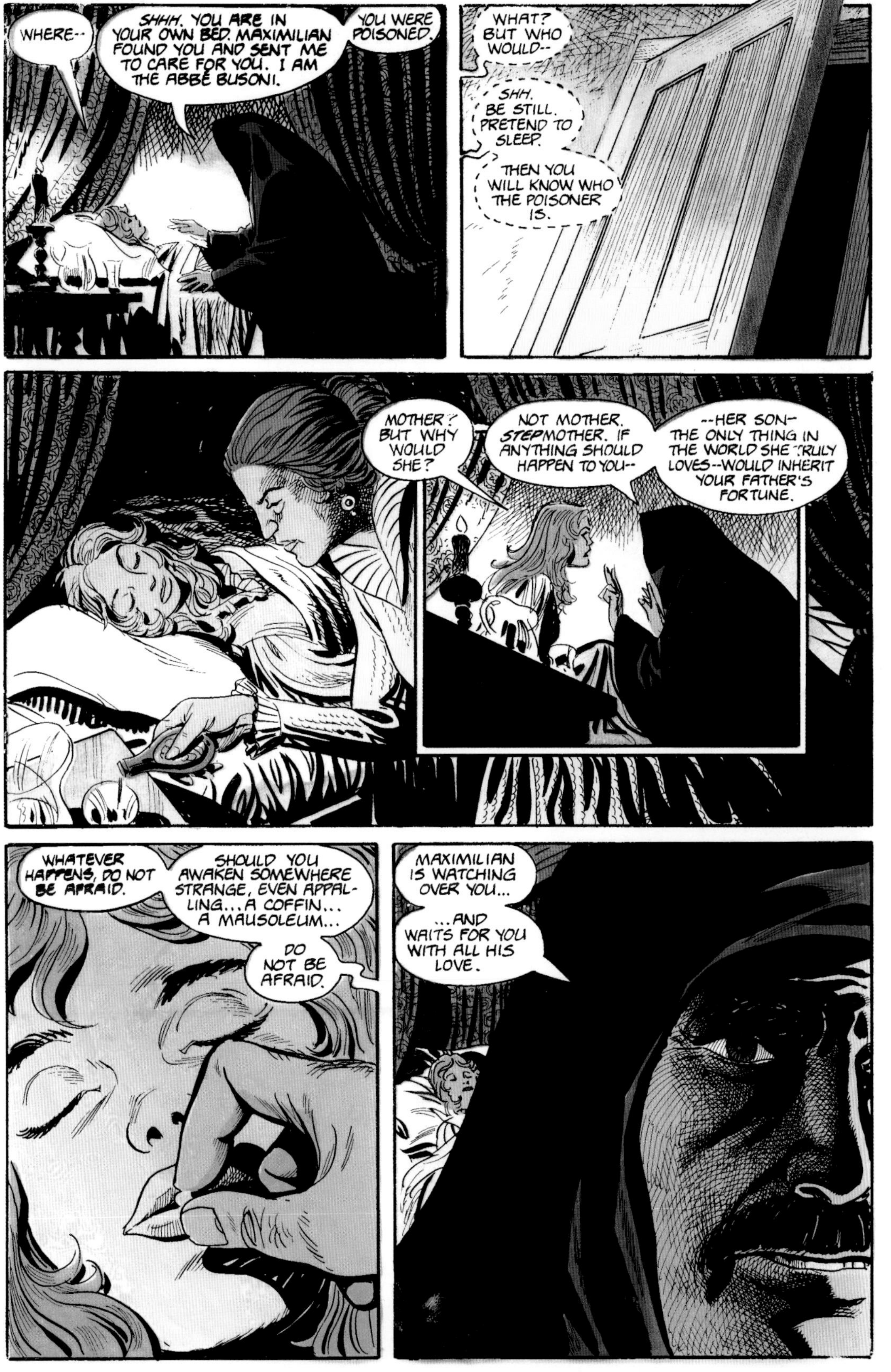
WHERE--
SHHH. YOU ARE IN YOUR OWN BED. MAXIMILIAN FOUND YOU AND SENT ME TO CARE FOR YOU. I AM THE ABBÉ BUSONI.
YOU WERE POISONED.
WHAT? BUT WHO WOULD--
SHH. BE STILL. PRETEND TO SLEEP.
THEN YOU WILL KNOW WHO THE POISONER IS.
MOTHER? BUT WHY WOULD SHE?
NOT MOTHER. STEPMOTHER. IF ANYTHING SHOULD HAPPEN TO YOU--
--HER SON-- THE ONLY THING IN THE WORLD SHE TRULY LOVES--WOULD INHERIT YOUR FATHER'S FORTUNE.
WHATEVER HAPPENS, DO NOT BE AFRAID.
SHOULD YOU AWAKEN SOMEWHERE STRANGE, EVEN APPALLING... A COFFIN... A MAUSOLEUM...
DO NOT BE AFRAID.
MAXIMILIAN IS WATCHING OVER YOU...
...AND WAITS FOR YOU WITH ALL HIS LOVE.

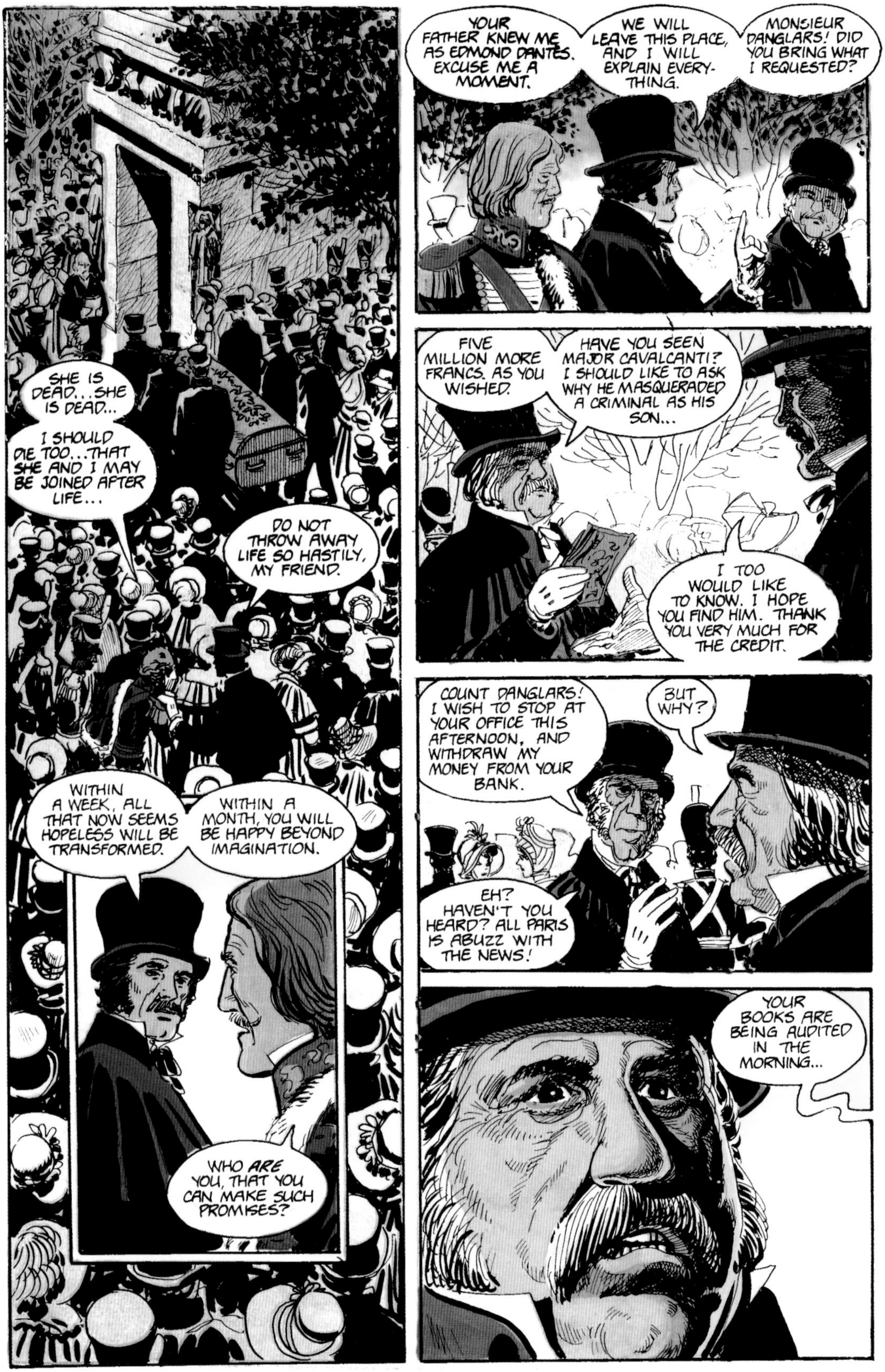
SHE IS DEAD...SHE IS DEAD...
I SHOULD DIE TOO...THAT SHE AND I MAY BE JOINED AFTER LIFE...
DO NOT THROW AWAY LIFE SO HASTILY, MY FRIEND.
WITHIN A WEEK, ALL THAT NOW SEEMS HOPELESS WILL BE TRANSFORMED.
WITHIN A MONTH, YOU WILL BE HAPPY BEYOND IMAGINATION.
WHO ARE YOU, THAT YOU CAN MAKE SUCH PROMISES?
YOUR FATHER KNEW ME AS EDMOND DANTÈS. EXCUSE ME A MOMENT.
WE WILL LEAVE THIS PLACE, AND I WILL EXPLAIN EVERY-THING.
MONSIEUR DANGLARS! DID YOU BRING WHAT I REQUESTED?
FIVE MILLION MORE FRANCS, AS YOU WISHED.
HAVE YOU SEEN MAJOR CAVALCANTI? I SHOULD LIKE TO ASK WHY HE MASQUERADED A CRIMINAL AS HIS SON...
I TOO WOULD LIKE TO KNOW. I HOPE YOU FIND HIM. THANK YOU VERY MUCH FOR THE CREDIT.
COUNT DANGLARS! I WISH TO STOP AT YOUR OFFICE THIS AFTERNOON, AND WITHDRAW MY MONEY FROM YOUR BANK.
BUT WHY?
EH? HAVEN'T YOU HEARD? ALL PARIS IS ABUZZ WITH THE NEWS!
YOUR BOOKS ARE BEING AUDITED IN THE MORNING...

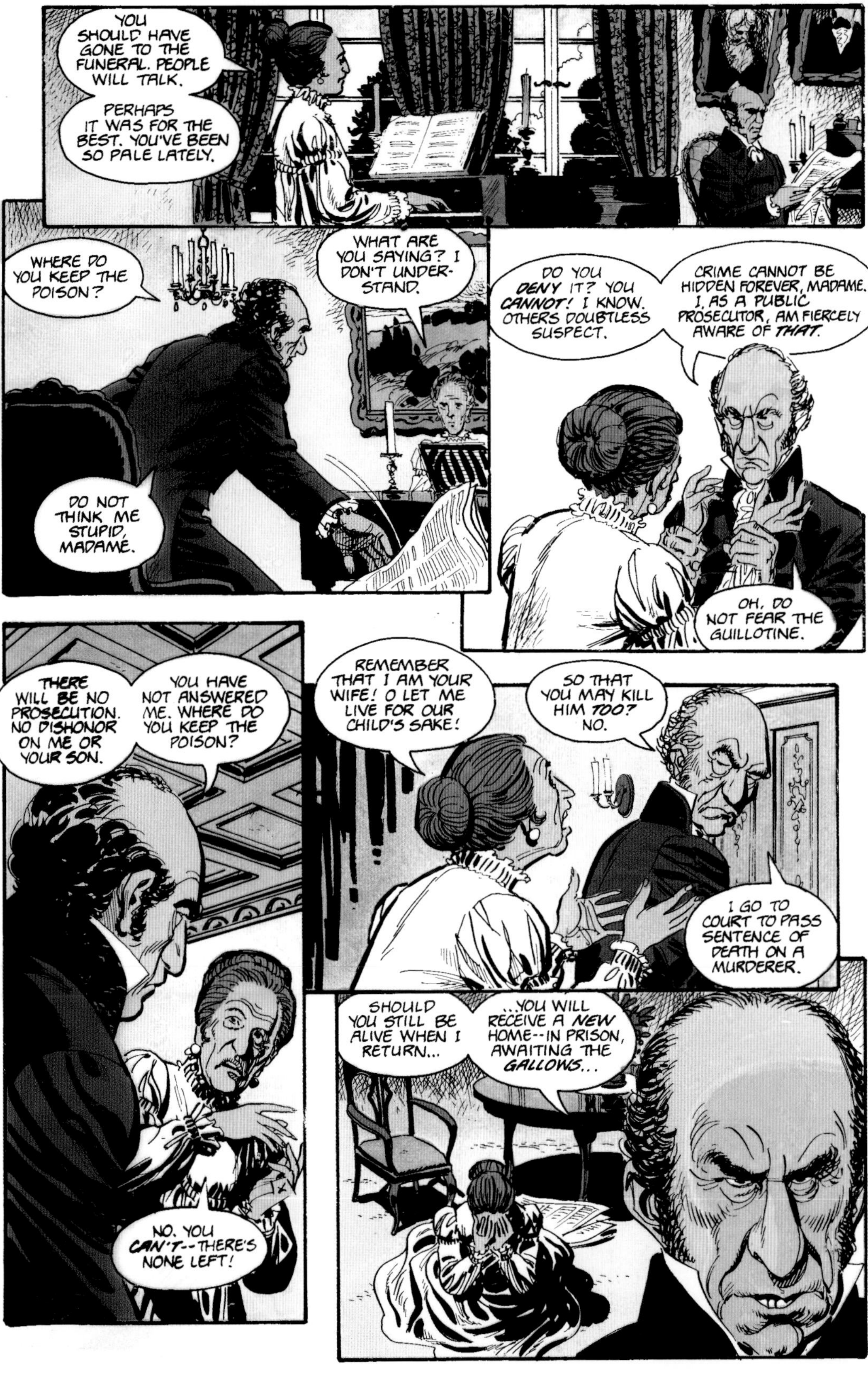
YOU SHOULD HAVE GONE TO THE FUNERAL. PEOPLE WILL TALK.
PERHAPS IT WAS FOR THE BEST. YOU'VE BEEN SO PALE LATELY.
WHERE DO YOU KEEP THE POISON?
WHAT ARE YOU SAYING? I DON'T UNDER-STAND.
DO NOT THINK ME STUPID, MADAME.
DO YOU DENY IT? YOU CANNOT! I KNOW. OTHERS DOUBTLESS SUSPECT.
CRIME CANNOT BE HIDDEN FOREVER, MADAME. I, AS A PUBLIC PROSECUTOR, AM FIERCELY AWARE OF THAT.
OH, DO NOT FEAR THE GUILLOTINE.
THERE WILL BE NO PROSECUTION. NO DISHONOR ON ME OR YOUR SON.
YOU HAVE NOT ANSWERED ME. WHERE DO YOU KEEP THE POISON?
NO. YOU CAN'T--THERE'S NONE LEFT!
REMEMBER THAT I AM YOUR WIFE! O LET ME LIVE FOR OUR CHILD'S SAKE!
SO THAT YOU MAY KILL HIM TOO? NO.
I GO TO COURT TO PASS SENTENCE OF DEATH ON A MURDERER.
SHOULD YOU STILL BE ALIVE WHEN I RETURN...
...YOU WILL RECEIVE A NEW HOME--IN PRISON, AWAITING THE GALLOWS...

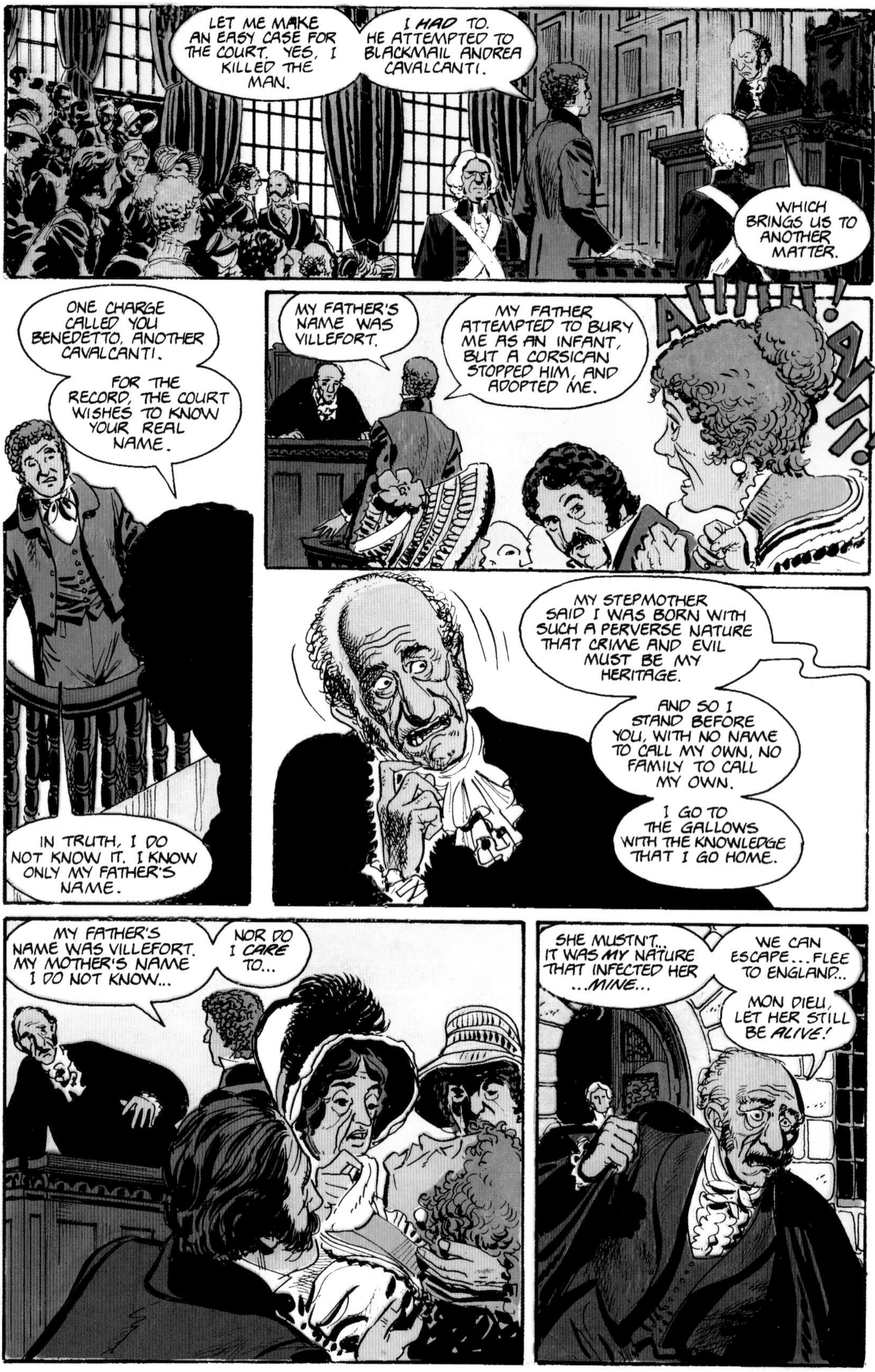
LET ME MAKE AN EASY CASE FOR THE COURT. YES, I KILLED THE MAN.
I HAD TO. HE ATTEMPTED TO BLACKMAIL ANDREA CAVALCANTI.
WHICH BRINGS US TO ANOTHER MATTER.
ONE CHARGE CALLED YOU BENEDETTO, ANOTHER CAVALCANTI.
FOR THE RECORD, THE COURT WISHES TO KNOW YOUR REAL NAME.
IN TRUTH, I DO NOT KNOW IT. I KNOW ONLY MY FATHER'S NAME.
MY FATHER'S NAME WAS VILLEFORT.
MY FATHER ATTEMPTED TO BURY ME AS AN INFANT, BUT A CORSICAN STOPPED HIM, AND ADOPTED ME.
AIIIII! AYIII!!
MY STEPMOTHER SAID I WAS BORN WITH SUCH A PERVERSE NATURE THAT CRIME AND EVIL MUST BE MY HERITAGE.
AND SO I STAND BEFORE YOU, WITH NO NAME TO CALL MY OWN, NO FAMILY TO CALL MY OWN.
I GO TO THE GALLOWS WITH THE KNOWLEDGE THAT I GO HOME.
MY FATHER'S NAME WAS VILLEFORT. MY MOTHER'S NAME I DO NOT KNOW...
NOR DO I CARE TO...
SHE MUSTN'T... IT WAS MY NATURE THAT INFECTED HER ...MINE...
WE CAN ESCAPE... FLEE TO ENGLAND...
MON DIEU, LET HER STILL BE ALIVE!

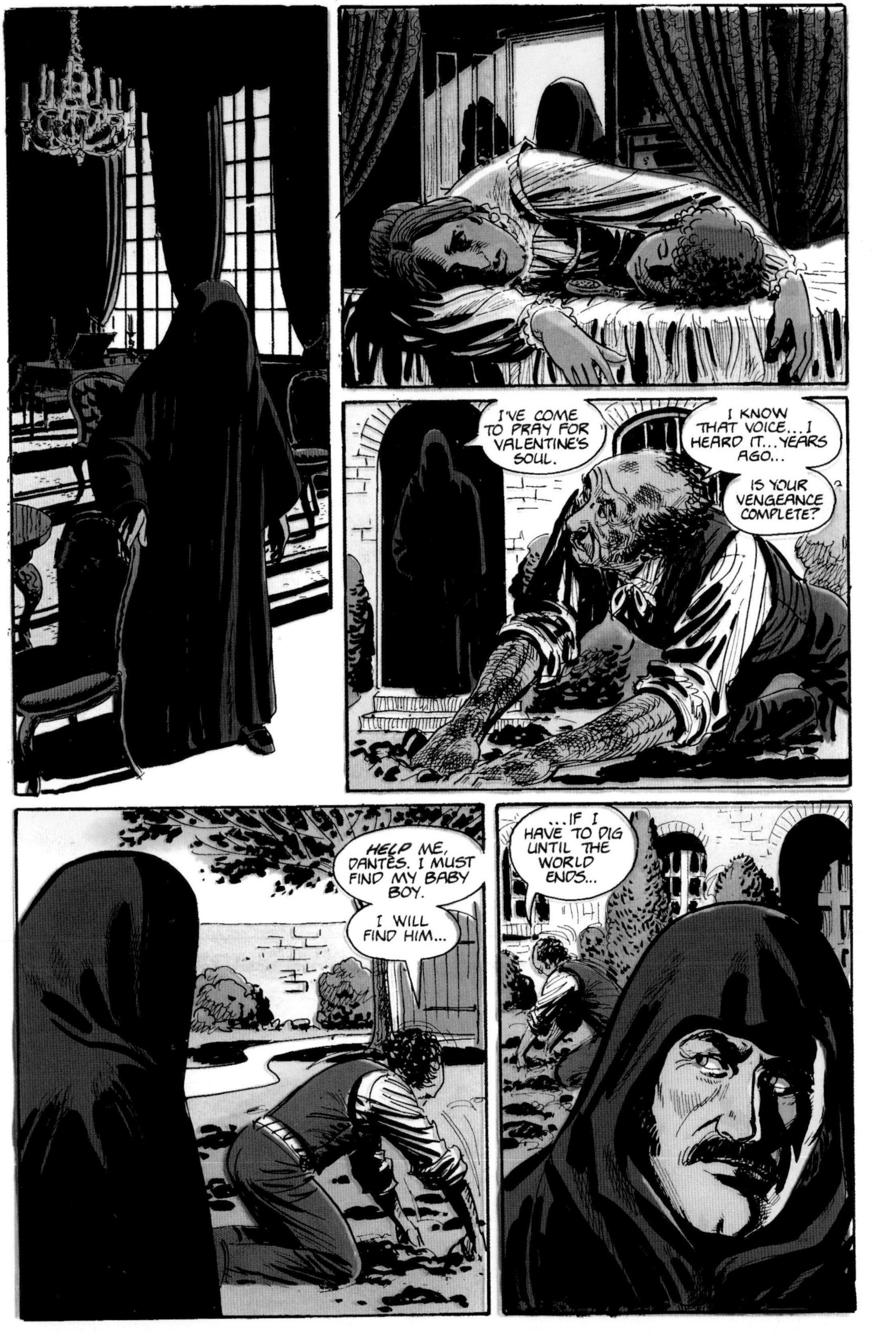
I'VE COME TO PRAY FOR VALENTINE'S SOUL.
I KNOW THAT VOICE... I HEARD IT... YEARS AGO...
IS YOUR VENGEANCE COMPLETE?
HELP ME, DANTÈS. I MUST FIND MY BABY BOY.
I WILL FIND HIM...
...IF I HAVE TO DIG UNTIL THE WORLD ENDS...

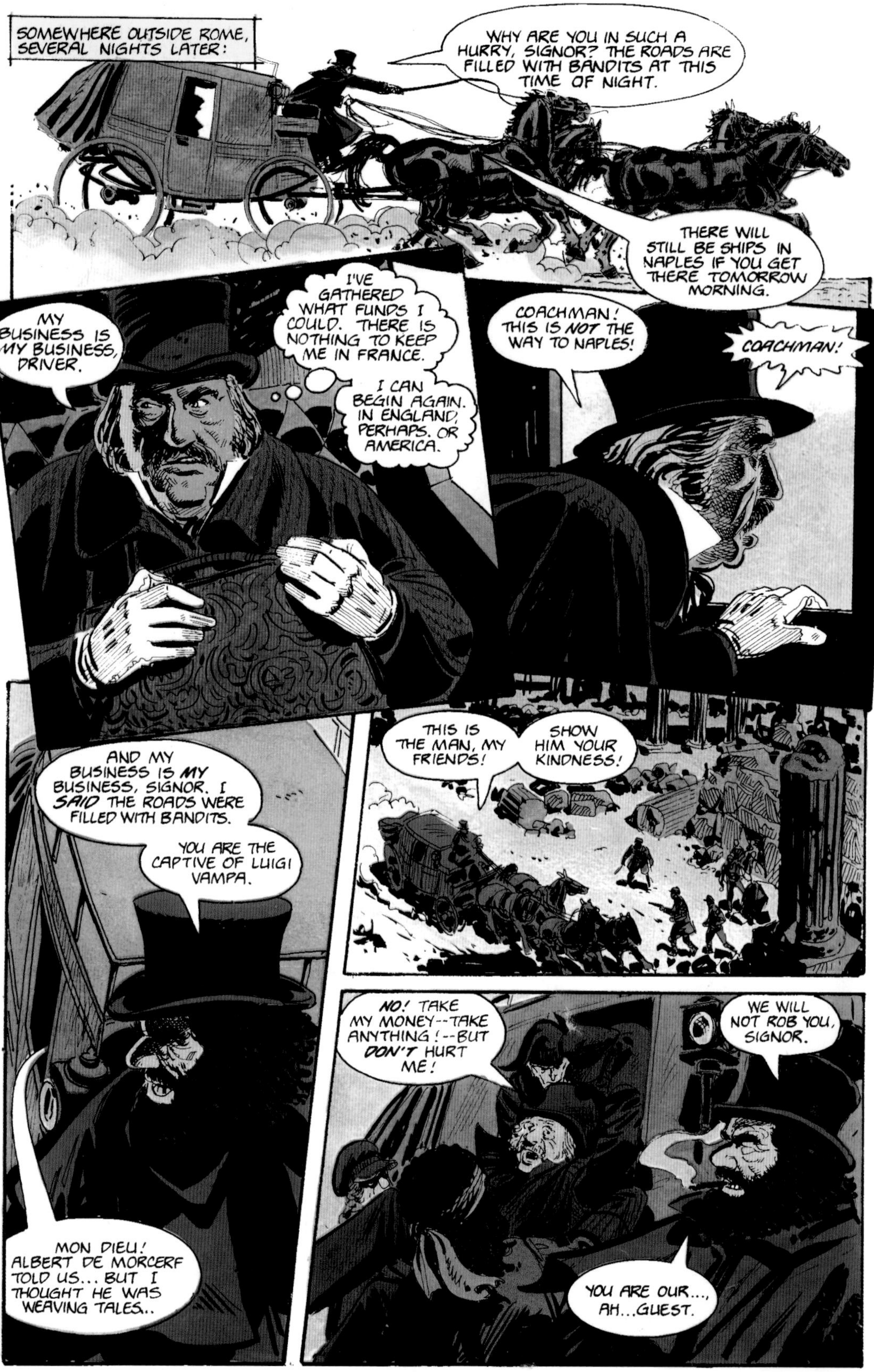
SOMEWHERE OUTSIDE ROME, SEVERAL NIGHTS LATER:
WHY ARE YOU IN SUCH A HURRY, SIGNOR? THE ROADS ARE FILLED WITH BANDITS AT THIS TIME OF NIGHT.
THERE WILL STILL BE SHIPS IN NAPLES IF YOU GET THERE TOMORROW MORNING.
MY BUSINESS IS MY BUSINESS, DRIVER.
I'VE GATHERED WHAT FUNDS I COULD. THERE IS NOTHING TO KEEP ME IN FRANCE.
I CAN BEGIN AGAIN. IN ENGLAND, PERHAPS. OR AMERICA.
COACHMAN! THIS IS NOT THE WAY TO NAPLES!
COACHMAN!
AND MY BUSINESS IS MY BUSINESS, SIGNOR. I SAID THE ROADS WERE FILLED WITH BANDITS.
YOU ARE THE CAPTIVE OF LUIGI VAMPA.
MON DIEU! ALBERT DE MORCERF TOLD US... BUT I THOUGHT HE WAS WEAVING TALES..
THIS IS THE MAN, MY FRIENDS!
SHOW HIM YOUR KINDNESS!
NO! TAKE MY MONEY--TAKE ANYTHING!--BUT DON'T HURT ME!
WE WILL NOT ROB YOU, SIGNOR.
YOU ARE OUR..., AH...GUEST.

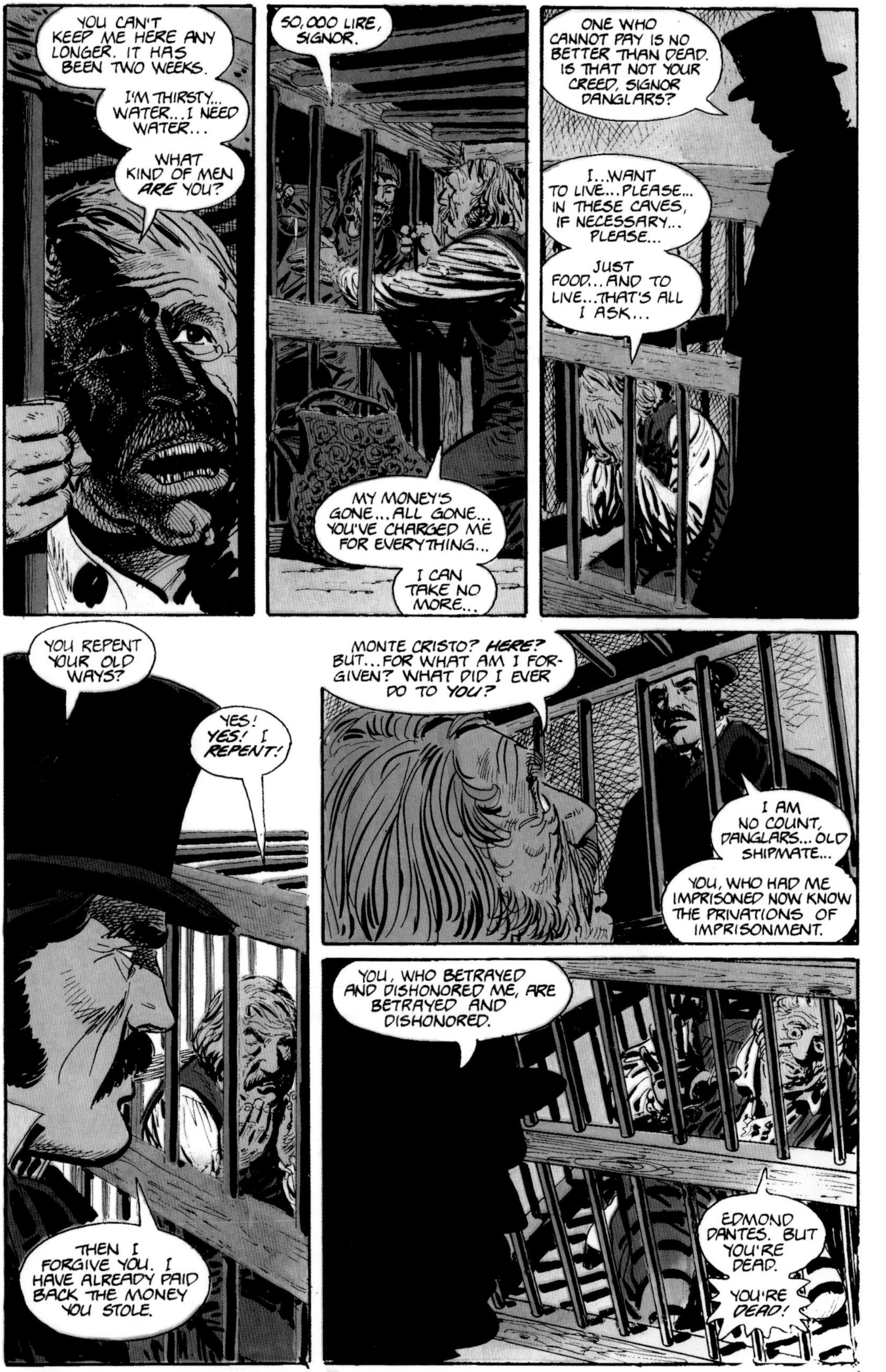
YOU CAN'T KEEP ME HERE ANY LONGER. IT HAS BEEN TWO WEEKS.
I'M THIRSTY... WATER... I NEED WATER...
WHAT KIND OF MEN *ARE* YOU?
50,000 LIRE, SIGNOR.
MY MONEY'S GONE... ALL GONE... YOU'VE CHARGED ME FOR EVERYTHING...
I CAN TAKE NO MORE...
ONE WHO CANNOT PAY IS NO BETTER THAN DEAD. IS THAT NOT YOUR CREED, SIGNOR DANGLARS?
I... WANT TO LIVE... PLEASE... IN THESE CAVES, IF NECESSARY... PLEASE...
JUST FOOD... AND TO LIVE... THAT'S ALL I ASK...
YOU REPENT YOUR OLD WAYS?
YES! *YES!* I *REPENT!*
THEN I FORGIVE YOU. I HAVE ALREADY PAID BACK THE MONEY YOU STOLE.
MONTE CRISTO? *HERE?* BUT... FOR WHAT AM I FORGIVEN? WHAT DID I EVER DO TO *YOU?*
I AM NO COUNT, DANGLARS... OLD SHIPMATE...
YOU, WHO HAD ME IMPRISONED NOW KNOW THE PRIVATIONS OF IMPRISONMENT.
YOU, WHO BETRAYED AND DISHONORED ME, ARE BETRAYED AND DISHONORED.
EDMOND DANTES. BUT YOU'RE DEAD.
YOU'RE *DEAD!*

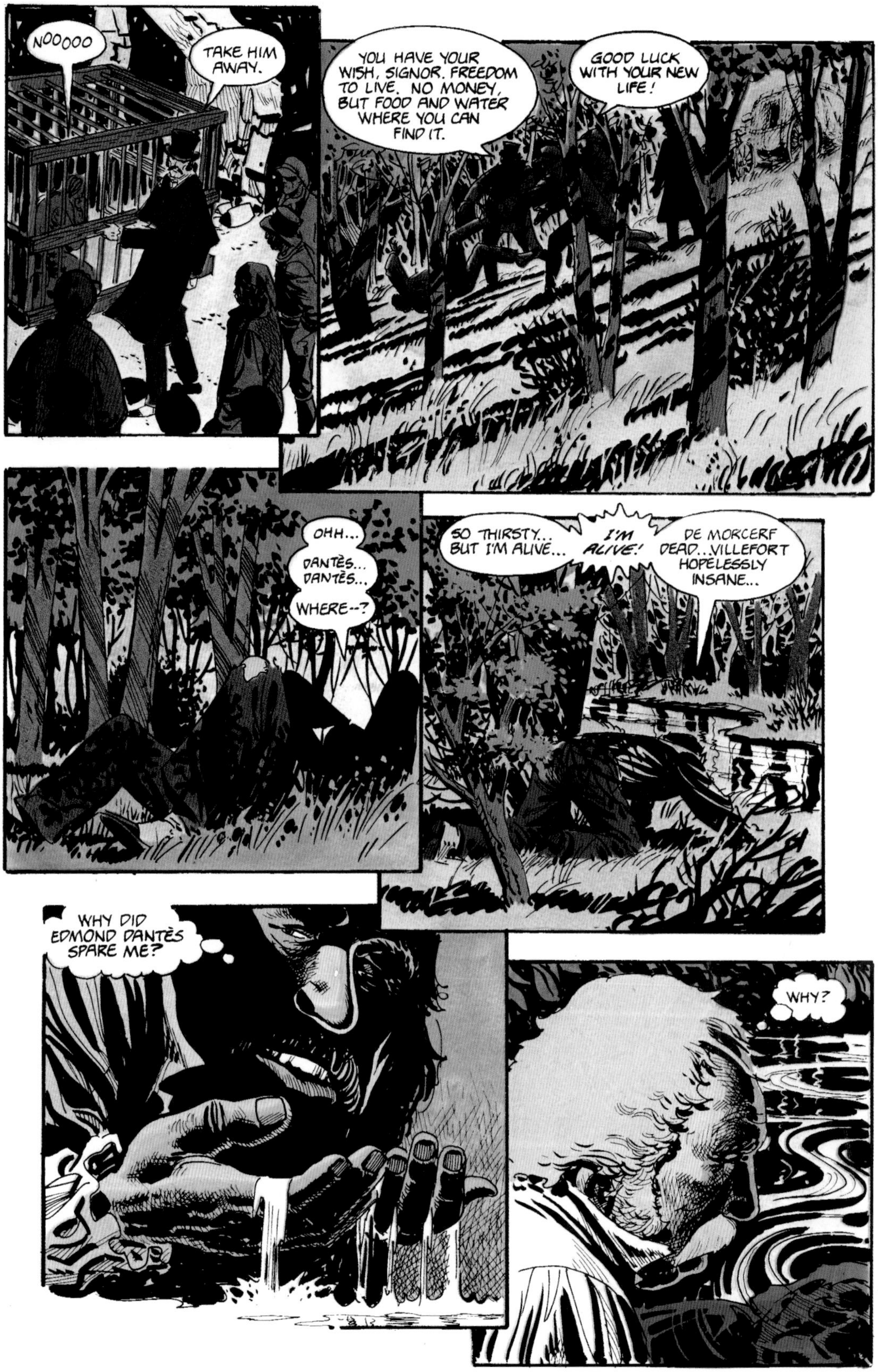
NOOOOO
TAKE HIM AWAY.
YOU HAVE YOUR WISH, SIGNOR. FREEDOM TO LIVE. NO MONEY, BUT FOOD AND WATER WHERE YOU CAN FIND IT.
GOOD LUCK WITH YOUR NEW LIFE!
OHH...
DANTÈS... DANTÈS...
WHERE--?
SO THIRSTY... BUT I'M ALIVE...
I'M ALIVE!
DE MORCERF DEAD...VILLEFORT HOPELESSLY INSANE...
WHY DID EDMOND DANTÈS SPARE ME?
WHY?

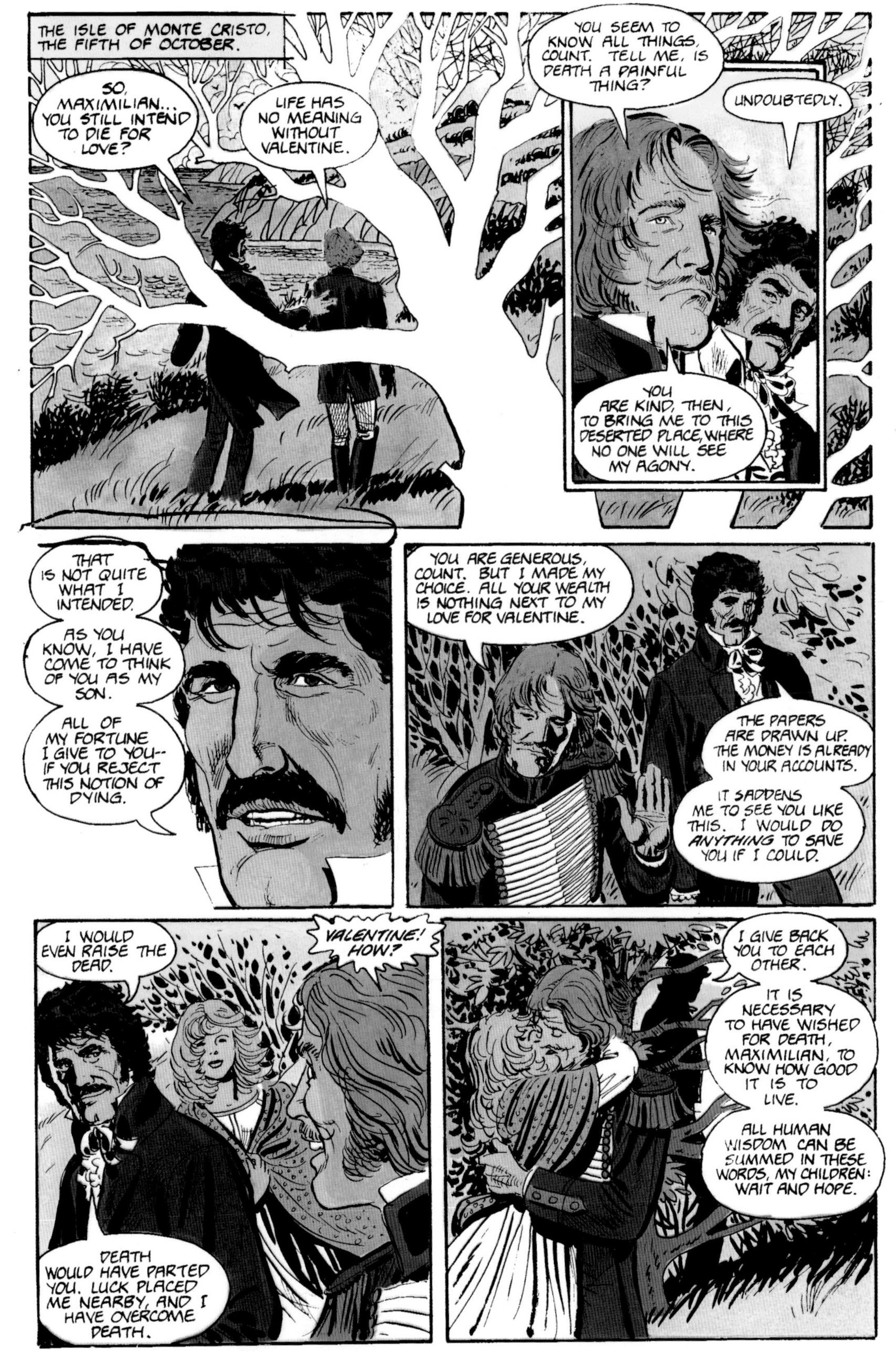
THE ISLE OF MONTE CRISTO, THE FIFTH OF OCTOBER.
SO, MAXIMILIAN... YOU STILL INTEND TO DIE FOR LOVE?
LIFE HAS NO MEANING WITHOUT VALENTINE.
YOU SEEM TO KNOW ALL THINGS, COUNT. TELL ME, IS DEATH A PAINFUL THING?
UNDOUBTEDLY.
YOU ARE KIND, THEN, TO BRING ME TO THIS DESERTED PLACE, WHERE NO ONE WILL SEE MY AGONY.
THAT IS NOT QUITE WHAT I INTENDED.
AS YOU KNOW, I HAVE COME TO THINK OF YOU AS MY SON.
ALL OF MY FORTUNE I GIVE TO YOU-- IF YOU REJECT THIS NOTION OF DYING.
YOU ARE GENEROUS, COUNT. BUT I MADE MY CHOICE. ALL YOUR WEALTH IS NOTHING NEXT TO MY LOVE FOR VALENTINE.
THE PAPERS ARE DRAWN UP. THE MONEY IS ALREADY IN YOUR ACCOUNTS.
IT SADDENS ME TO SEE YOU LIKE THIS. I WOULD DO *ANYTHING* TO SAVE YOU IF I COULD.
I WOULD EVEN RAISE THE DEAD.
VALENTINE! HOW?
DEATH WOULD HAVE PARTED YOU. LUCK PLACED ME NEARBY, AND I HAVE OVERCOME DEATH.
I GIVE BACK YOU TO EACH OTHER.
IT IS NECESSARY TO HAVE WISHED FOR DEATH, MAXIMILIAN, TO KNOW HOW GOOD IT IS TO LIVE.
ALL HUMAN WISDOM CAN BE SUMMED IN THESE WORDS, MY CHILDREN: WAIT AND HOPE.

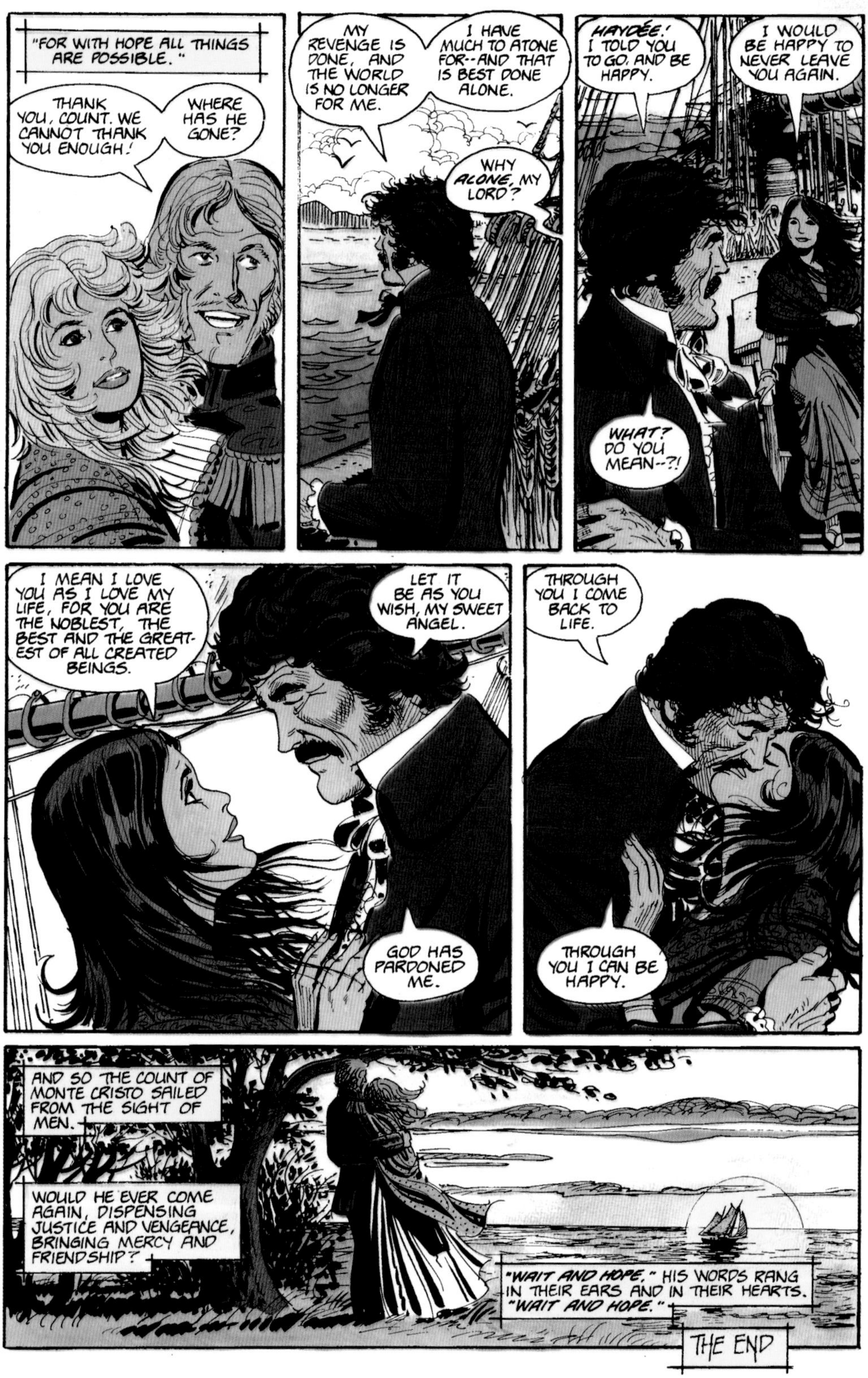
"FOR WITH HOPE ALL THINGS ARE POSSIBLE."
THANK YOU, COUNT. WE CANNOT THANK YOU ENOUGH!
WHERE HAS HE GONE?
MY REVENGE IS DONE, AND THE WORLD IS NO LONGER FOR ME.
I HAVE MUCH TO ATONE FOR--AND THAT IS BEST DONE ALONE.
WHY ALONE, MY LORD?
HAYDÉE! I TOLD YOU TO GO, AND BE HAPPY.
I WOULD BE HAPPY TO NEVER LEAVE YOU AGAIN.
WHAT? DO YOU MEAN--?!
I MEAN I LOVE YOU AS I LOVE MY LIFE, FOR YOU ARE THE NOBLEST, THE BEST AND THE GREATEST OF ALL CREATED BEINGS.
LET IT BE AS YOU WISH, MY SWEET ANGEL.
GOD HAS PARDONED ME.
THROUGH YOU I COME BACK TO LIFE.
THROUGH YOU I CAN BE HAPPY.
AND SO THE COUNT OF MONTE CRISTO SAILED FROM THE SIGHT OF MEN.
WOULD HE EVER COME AGAIN, DISPENSING JUSTICE AND VENGEANCE, BRINGING MERCY AND FRIENDSHIP?
"WAIT AND HOPE," HIS WORDS RANG IN THEIR EARS AND IN THEIR HEARTS. "WAIT AND HOPE."
THE END

WATCH OUT FOR
PAPERCUT Z ™

Welcome to the eighth Papercutz edition of CLASSICS ILLUSTRATED. I'm Jim Salicrup, your friendly, flu-fighting Editor-in-Chief. You know, I really hope you're enjoying our CLASSICS ILLUSTRATED series as much as we are. These particular adaptations of Stories by the World's Greatest Authors were originally published by the fine folks at First Comics Publishing, and unfortunately may have been too far ahead of their time. They were created for bookstore distribution back when bookstores would shelve such serious, groundbreaking graphic novels such as Will Eisner's *A Contract with God* and Art Spiegelman's *Maus* in the humor section along with the latest collections of *Garfield* and *Ziggy*. Times sure have changed, and graphic novels are finally getting the respect, and distribution, they deserve.

When Papercutz publisher Terry Nantier and I decided to bring back CLAS-SICS ILLUSTRATED, we were thinking that the series would be especially appealing to libraries and schools. Well, turns out we were right! Here's just a couple of reviews from two of the most prestigious magazines which cover the educational market regarding CLASSICS ILLUSTRATED #5 "Hamlet":

"Outstanding... the core of the play is maintained, showing the inter-family strife and the angst of Hamlet as he seeks revenge for the death of his father... illustrated in a way to draw the student into the darkness of the play." — **Library Media Connection**

"...The retelling puts the play's original language center stage as events unfold in the vividly detailed panels. A panorama of changing emotions play across the characters' expressive faces and are also revealed through their body language and echoed in the atmospheric backdrops. Fight scenes are presented with flair, the ghost is particularly dramatic, and the image of the drowned garland-strewn Ophelia is unforgettable."
— **School Library Journal**

How cool is that? Yet no matter how many such rave reviews CLASSICS ILLUSTRATED is currently garnering, the coolest thing is that each adaptation is a great graphic novel on its own, adapted by the Greatest Writers and Artists in Comics!

(Speaking of which, check out the following preview of the all-new adaptation of Robert Louis Stevenson's *Treasure Island* by David Chauvel, writer; Fred Simon, artist; and Jean-Luc Simon, colorist. It's absolutely beautiful, and will be coming your way in CLASSICS ILLUSTRATED DELUXE #5.)

Thanks, *Jim*

SPECIAL PREVIEW OF CLASSICS ILLUSTRATED DELUXE #5 "TREASURE ISLAND"...

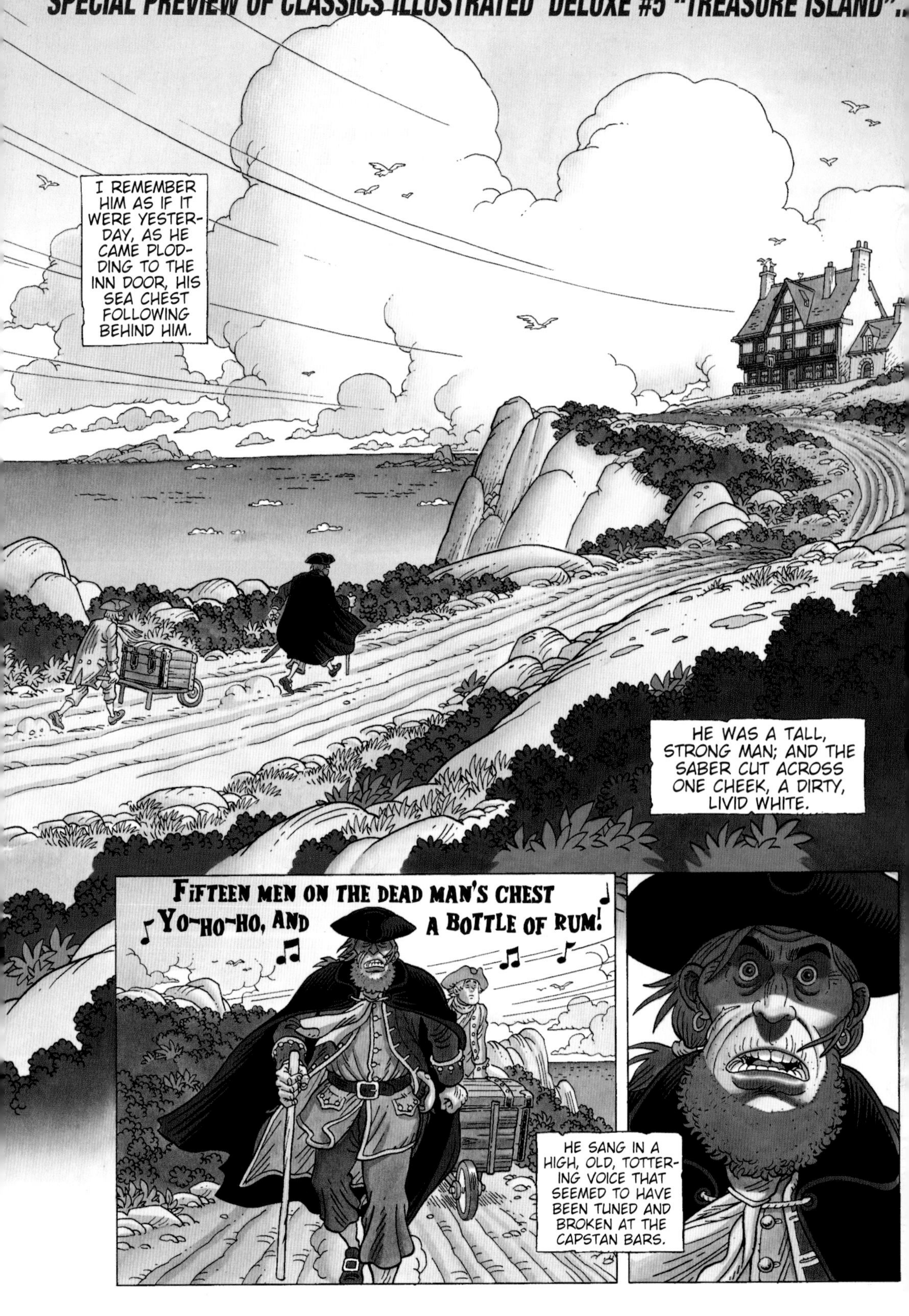
I REMEMBER HIM AS IF IT WERE YESTERDAY, AS HE CAME PLODDING TO THE INN DOOR, HIS SEA CHEST FOLLOWING BEHIND HIM.
HE WAS A TALL, STRONG MAN; AND THE SABER CUT ACROSS ONE CHEEK, A DIRTY, LIVID WHITE.
FIFTEEN MEN ON THE DEAD MAN'S CHEST
YO-HO-HO, AND A BOTTLE OF RUM!
HE SANG IN A HIGH, OLD, TOTTERING VOICE THAT SEEMED TO HAVE BEEN TUNED AND BROKEN AT THE CAPSTAN BARS.

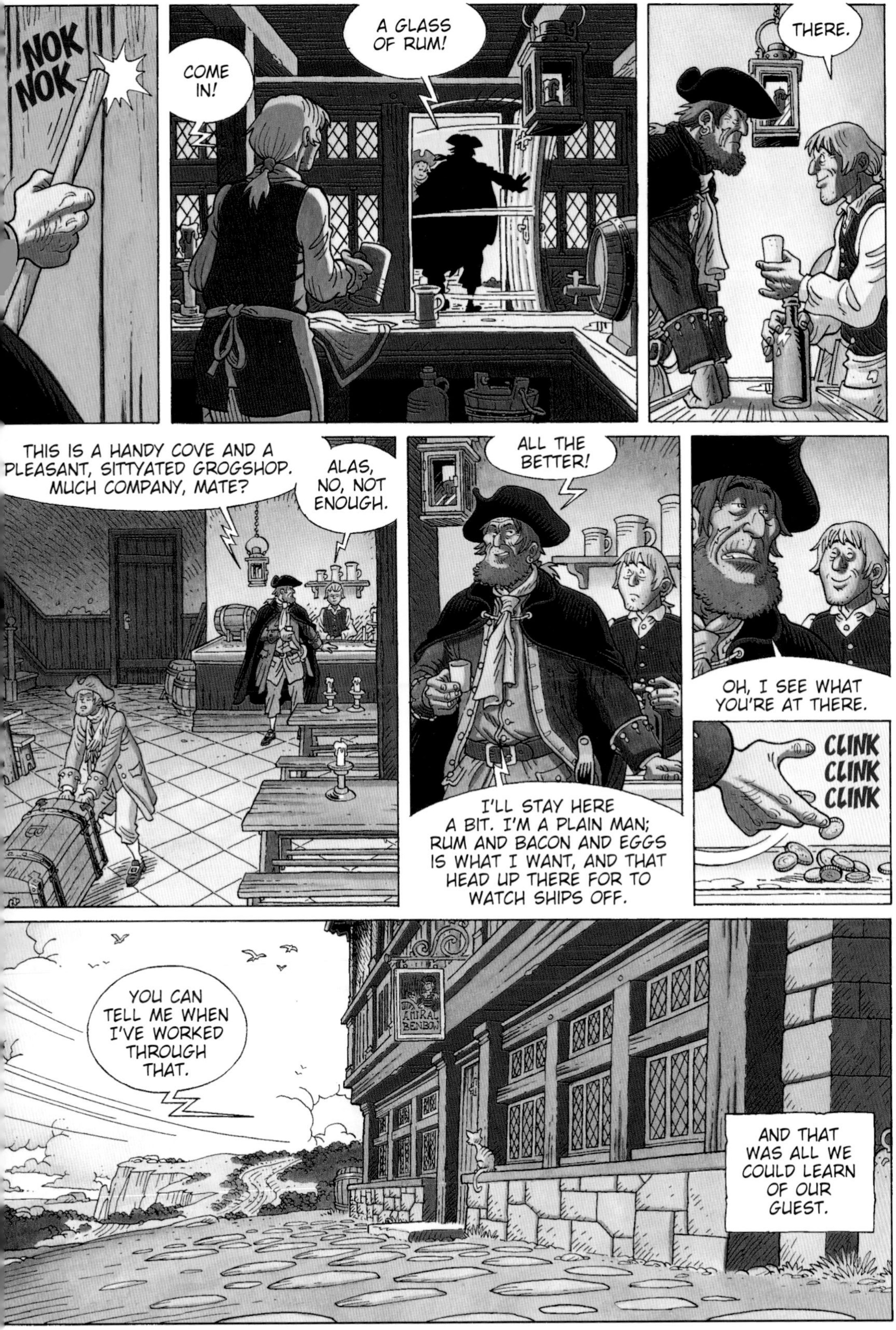
NOK NOK
COME IN!
A GLASS OF RUM!
THERE.
THIS IS A HANDY COVE AND A PLEASANT, SITTYATED GROGSHOP. MUCH COMPANY, MATE?
ALAS, NO, NOT ENOUGH.
ALL THE BETTER!
I'LL STAY HERE A BIT. I'M A PLAIN MAN; RUM AND BACON AND EGGS IS WHAT I WANT, AND THAT HEAD UP THERE FOR TO WATCH SHIPS OFF.
OH, I SEE WHAT YOU'RE AT THERE.
CLINK CLINK CLINK
YOU CAN TELL ME WHEN I'VE WORKED THROUGH THAT.
ADMIRAL BENBOW
AND THAT WAS ALL WE COULD LEARN OF OUR GUEST.

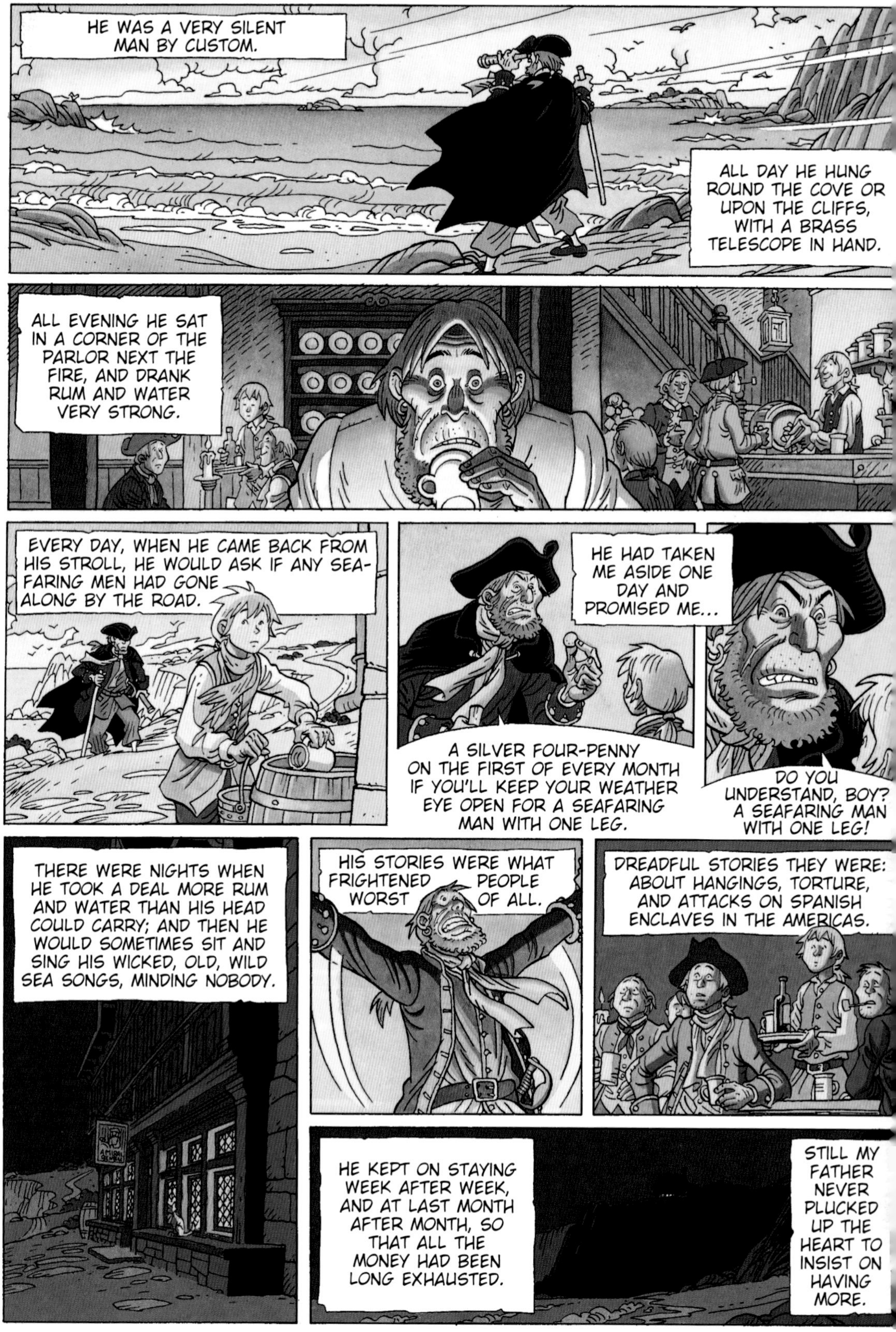
HE WAS A VERY SILENT MAN BY CUSTOM.
ALL DAY HE HUNG ROUND THE COVE OR UPON THE CLIFFS, WITH A BRASS TELESCOPE IN HAND.
ALL EVENING HE SAT IN A CORNER OF THE PARLOR NEXT THE FIRE, AND DRANK RUM AND WATER VERY STRONG.
EVERY DAY, WHEN HE CAME BACK FROM HIS STROLL, HE WOULD ASK IF ANY SEA-FARING MEN HAD GONE ALONG BY THE ROAD.
HE HAD TAKEN ME ASIDE ONE DAY AND PROMISED ME...
A SILVER FOUR-PENNY ON THE FIRST OF EVERY MONTH IF YOU'LL KEEP YOUR WEATHER EYE OPEN FOR A SEAFARING MAN WITH ONE LEG.
DO YOU UNDERSTAND, BOY? A SEAFARING MAN WITH ONE LEG!
THERE WERE NIGHTS WHEN HE TOOK A DEAL MORE RUM AND WATER THAN HIS HEAD COULD CARRY; AND THEN HE WOULD SOMETIMES SIT AND SING HIS WICKED, OLD, WILD SEA SONGS, MINDING NOBODY.
HIS STORIES WERE WHAT FRIGHTENED PEOPLE WORST OF ALL.
DREADFUL STORIES THEY WERE: ABOUT HANGINGS, TORTURE, AND ATTACKS ON SPANISH ENCLAVES IN THE AMERICAS.
HE KEPT ON STAYING WEEK AFTER WEEK, AND AT LAST MONTH AFTER MONTH, SO THAT ALL THE MONEY HAD BEEN LONG EXHAUSTED.
STILL MY FATHER NEVER PLUCKED UP THE HEART TO INSIST ON HAVING MORE.

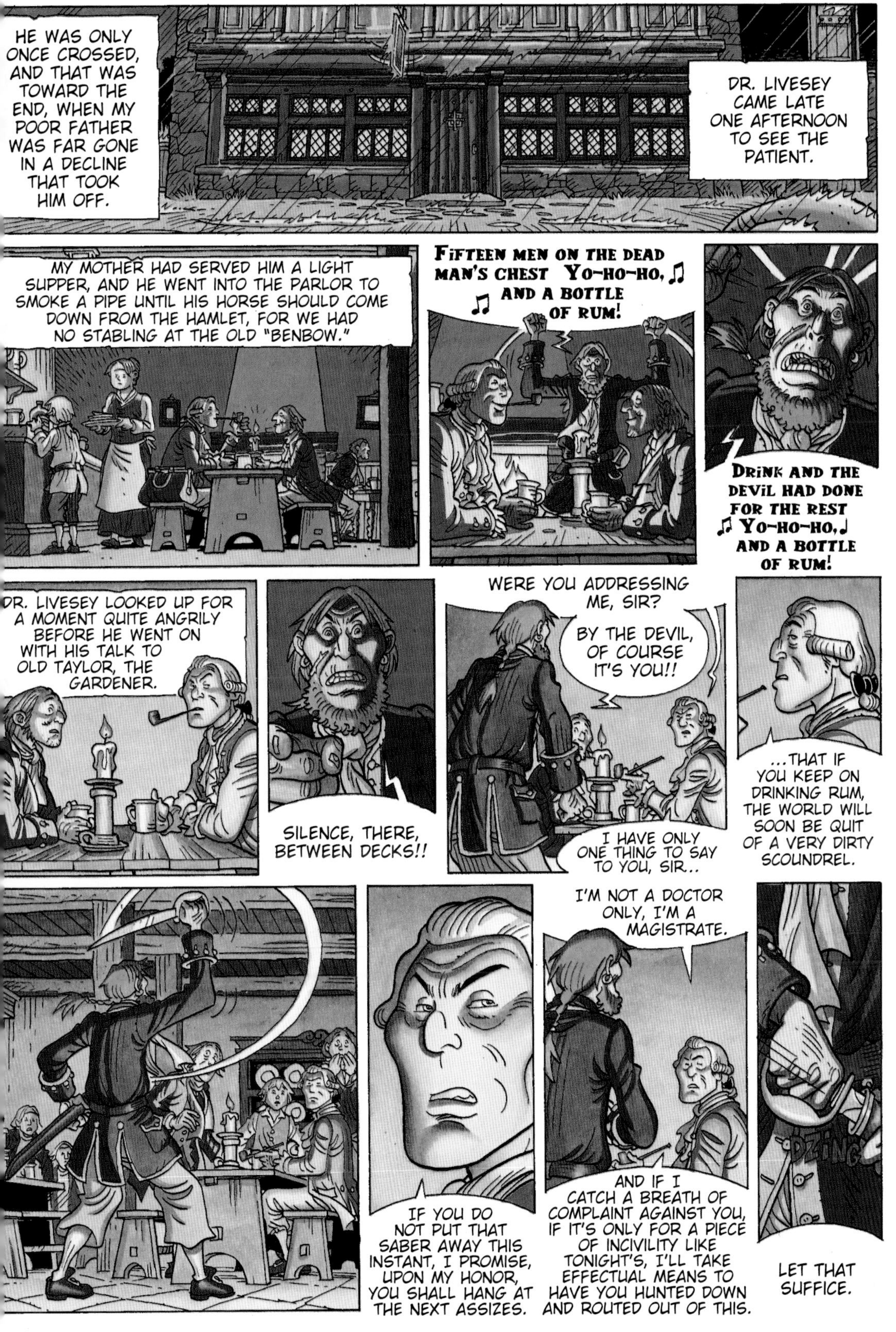
HE WAS ONLY ONCE CROSSED, AND THAT WAS TOWARD THE END, WHEN MY POOR FATHER WAS FAR GONE IN A DECLINE THAT TOOK HIM OFF.
DR. LIVESEY CAME LATE ONE AFTERNOON TO SEE THE PATIENT.
MY MOTHER HAD SERVED HIM A LIGHT SUPPER, AND HE WENT INTO THE PARLOR TO SMOKE A PIPE UNTIL HIS HORSE SHOULD COME DOWN FROM THE HAMLET, FOR WE HAD NO STABLING AT THE OLD "BENBOW."
FIFTEEN MEN ON THE DEAD MAN'S CHEST YO-HO-HO, ♫ ♫ AND A BOTTLE OF RUM!
DRINK AND THE DEVIL HAD DONE FOR THE REST ♫ YO-HO-HO, ♩ AND A BOTTLE OF RUM!
DR. LIVESEY LOOKED UP FOR A MOMENT QUITE ANGRILY BEFORE HE WENT ON WITH HIS TALK TO OLD TAYLOR, THE GARDENER.
SILENCE, THERE, BETWEEN DECKS!!
WERE YOU ADDRESSING ME, SIR?
BY THE DEVIL, OF COURSE IT'S YOU!!
I HAVE ONLY ONE THING TO SAY TO YOU, SIR...
...THAT IF YOU KEEP ON DRINKING RUM, THE WORLD WILL SOON BE QUIT OF A VERY DIRTY SCOUNDREL.
IF YOU DO NOT PUT THAT SABER AWAY THIS INSTANT, I PROMISE, UPON MY HONOR, YOU SHALL HANG AT THE NEXT ASSIZES.
I'M NOT A DOCTOR ONLY, I'M A MAGISTRATE.
AND IF I CATCH A BREATH OF COMPLAINT AGAINST YOU, IF IT'S ONLY FOR A PIECE OF INCIVILITY LIKE TONIGHT'S, I'LL TAKE EFFECTUAL MEANS TO HAVE YOU HUNTED DOWN AND ROUTED OUT OF THIS.
DZING
LET THAT SUFFICE.

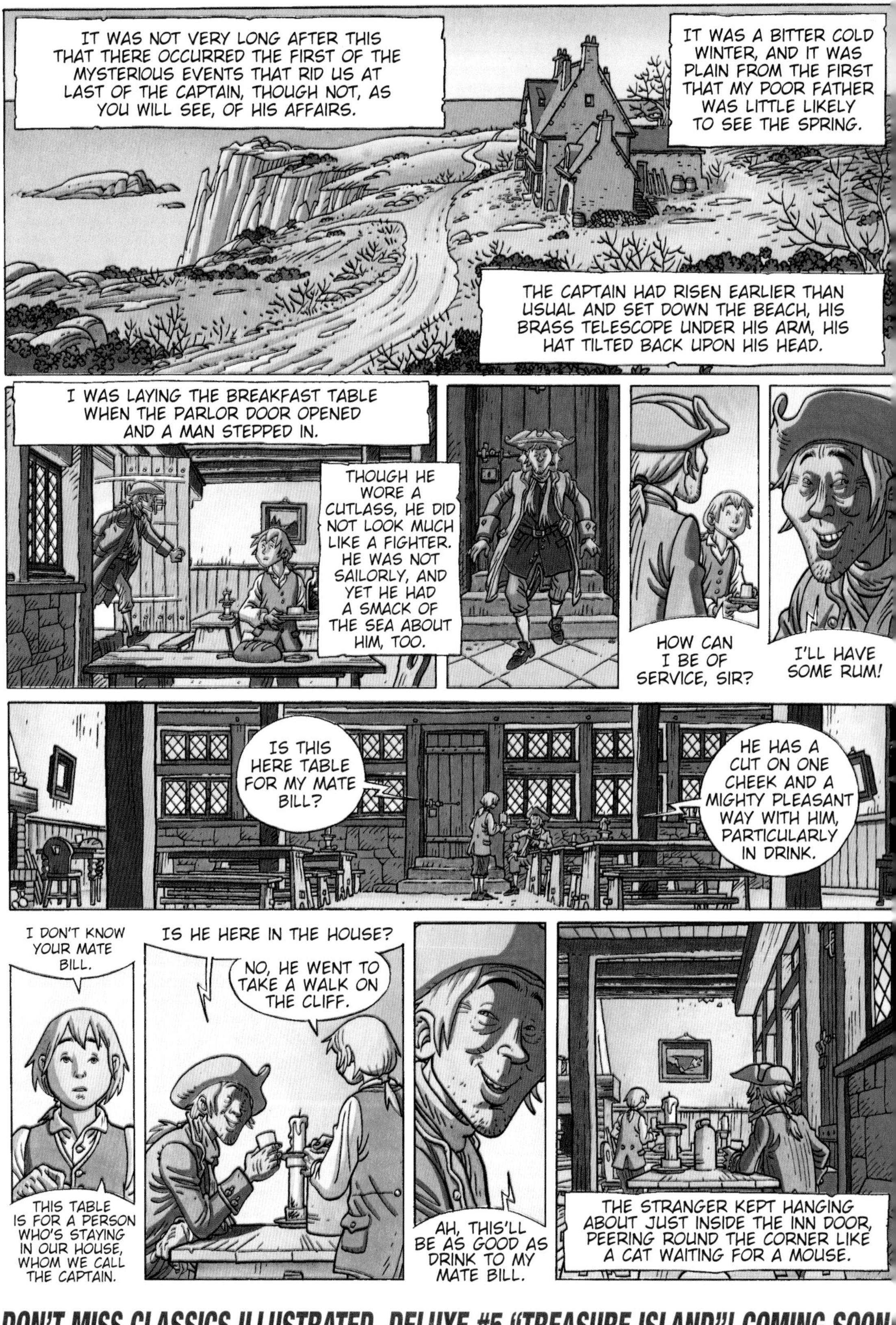
IT WAS NOT VERY LONG AFTER THIS THAT THERE OCCURRED THE FIRST OF THE MYSTERIOUS EVENTS THAT RID US AT LAST OF THE CAPTAIN, THOUGH NOT, AS YOU WILL SEE, OF HIS AFFAIRS.
IT WAS A BITTER COLD WINTER, AND IT WAS PLAIN FROM THE FIRST THAT MY POOR FATHER WAS LITTLE LIKELY TO SEE THE SPRING.
THE CAPTAIN HAD RISEN EARLIER THAN USUAL AND SET DOWN THE BEACH, HIS BRASS TELESCOPE UNDER HIS ARM, HIS HAT TILTED BACK UPON HIS HEAD.
I WAS LAYING THE BREAKFAST TABLE WHEN THE PARLOR DOOR OPENED AND A MAN STEPPED IN.
THOUGH HE WORE A CUTLASS, HE DID NOT LOOK MUCH LIKE A FIGHTER. HE WAS NOT SAILORLY, AND YET HE HAD A SMACK OF THE SEA ABOUT HIM, TOO.
HOW CAN I BE OF SERVICE, SIR?
I'LL HAVE SOME RUM!
IS THIS HERE TABLE FOR MY MATE BILL?
HE HAS A CUT ON ONE CHEEK AND A MIGHTY PLEASANT WAY WITH HIM, PARTICULARLY IN DRINK.
I DON'T KNOW YOUR MATE BILL.
THIS TABLE IS FOR A PERSON WHO'S STAYING IN OUR HOUSE, WHOM WE CALL THE CAPTAIN.
IS HE HERE IN THE HOUSE?
NO, HE WENT TO TAKE A WALK ON THE CLIFF.
AH, THIS'LL BE AS GOOD AS DRINK TO MY MATE BILL.
THE STRANGER KEPT HANGING ABOUT JUST INSIDE THE INN DOOR, PEERING ROUND THE CORNER LIKE A CAT WAITING FOR A MOUSE.

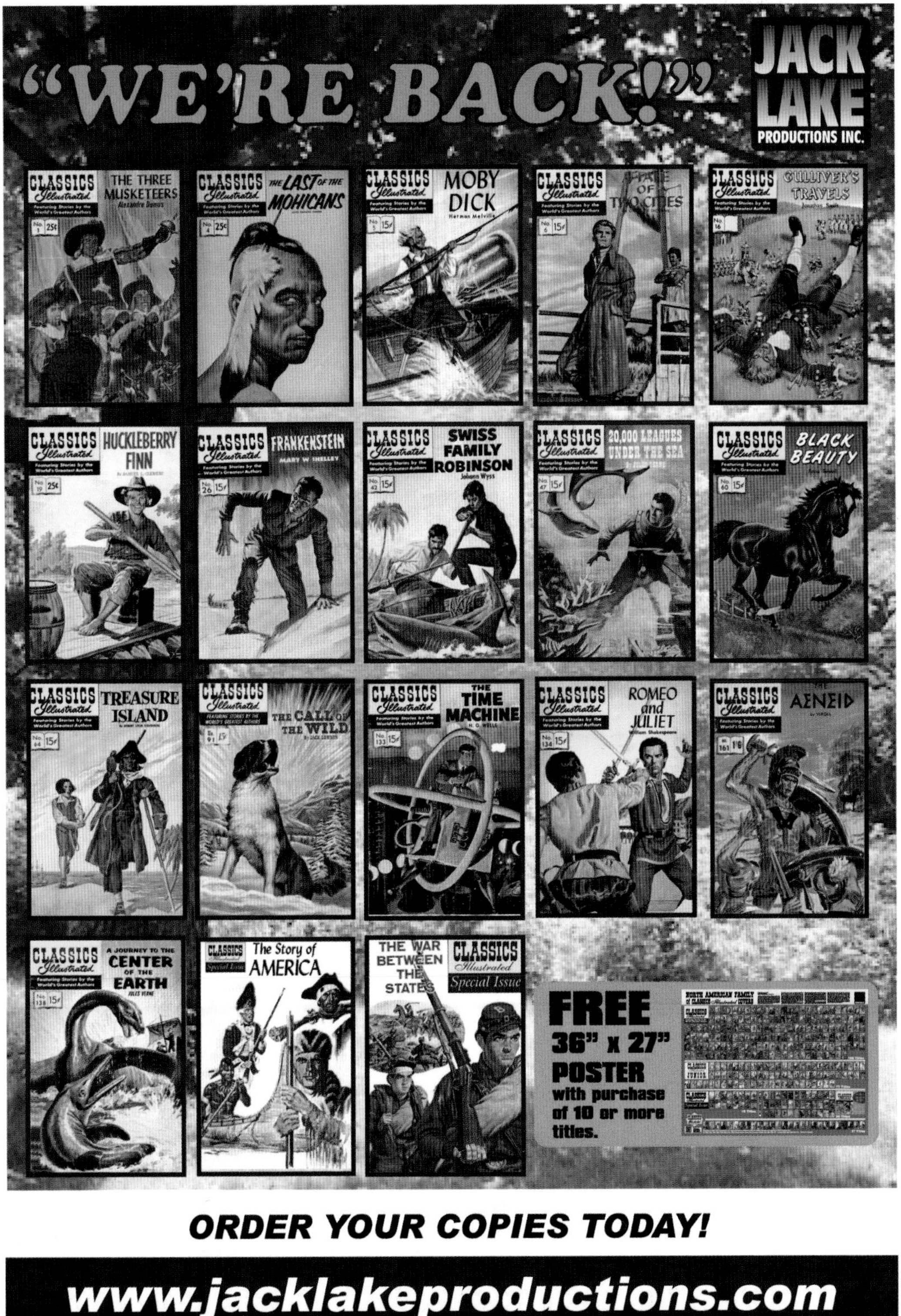
"WE'RE BACK!"
JACK LAKE
PRODUCTIONS INC.
CLASSICS Illustrated
THE THREE MUSKETEERS
THE LAST OF THE MOHICANS
MOBY DICK
Herman Melville
GULLIVER'S TRAVELS
HUCKLEBERRY FINN
FRANKENSTEIN
MARY W. SHELLEY
SWISS FAMILY ROBINSON
Johann Wyss
20,000 LEAGUES UNDER THE SEA
BLACK BEAUTY
TREASURE ISLAND
THE CALL OF THE WILD
THE TIME MACHINE
H. G. WELLS
ROMEO and JULIET
William Shakespeare
ΑΕΝΕΙΔ
A JOURNEY TO THE CENTER OF THE EARTH
JULES VERNE
The Story of AMERICA
Special Issue
THE WAR BETWEEN THE STATES
CLASSICS Illustrated Special Issue
FREE
36" x 27"
POSTER
with purchase of 10 or more titles.

ALEXANDRE DUMAS

Alexandre Dumas was born in Villers-Cotterets, France, on July 24, 1802, the son of a mulatto general who had fought alongside Napoleon. General Dumas, however, fell out of favor with the French emperor, and died virtually penniless. Young Dumas's education was limited, but, upon his move to Paris in 1823, his graceful handwriting brought him a job in the secretariat of the Duc d'Orleans, later the King of France. In 1824, he fathered a son know as Alexander Dumas *fils* (who also became a successful novelist and playwright). Dumas's first play, *Henri III et sa Cour* (1829), opened at the Comédie-Française before an enthusiastic audience. He achieved further fame with other theatrical triumphs: *Antony* (1831), *La Tour de Nesle* (1832), and *Kean* (1836). Dumas's grand, melodramatic historical romances began to appear around 1840, as serialized newspaper installments that were later collected into books. To assist in research, Dumas assembled a number of collaborators to create what they called his "factory." They combed newspapers, magazines, and books for suitably exciting plots, a practice that exposed Dumas to charges of pilfering history and pilfering from other writers. Also, Dumas's works were so massive and appeared with such rapidity that critics began to suspect they had been ghostwritten. Even had the accusations been proven, it is unlikely that French readers would have taken notice: Dumas's books were among the bestsellers of the time. The successes of *The Three Musketeers* (1844-1845), *Twenty Years After* (1845), *The Count of Monte Cristo* (1844), and *The Man in the Iron Mask* (1848-1850), brought Dumas wealth as well as glory. In 1848, Dumas married his mistress, Ida Ferrier, and built his own Château de Monte Cristo; more than 600 attended the housewarming dinner. Flamboyant and reckless, Dumas spent with abandon, socializing with royalty and the elite of Paris. Soon bankrupt, he fled to Belgium in 1851 to escape creditors. Dumas died on December 5, 1870; ever-romantic, he said of his death, "I shall tell her a story, and she will be kind to me."

Dan Spiegle was born in Washington state in 1920. During World War II, Spiegle served in the U.S. Navy; he drew for a base newspaper, and painted insignias on fighter and torpedo planes in the South Pacific. After the war, he attended the Chouinard Art Institute in Los Angeles, majoring in illustration. In 1950, Spiegle was selected to create the *Hopalong Cassidy* comic strip, which went on to appear in some 200 newspapers across the country. Spiegle joined Western Publishing in 1956, where he adapted a number of Disney movies and television shows. His credits include *Maverick, Lawman, Rifleman, Rawhide, Spin and Marty, Sea Hunt, Green Hornet,* and *Space Family Robinson,* the inspiration for the television series Lost in Space.

Steven Grant was born in Madison, Wisconsin, in 1953. He graduated from the University of Wisconsin, where he studied communication arts and comparative mythology. Grant's comics credits include *Twilight Man, Whisper, Punisher, The Incredible Hulk,* and *The Avengers.* The former editor-in-chief of the Velvet Light Trap Review of Cinema, Grant has written music criticism for Trouser Press, and has contributed to several books on popular culture, including *Close-Ups* and *The Rock Yearbook.* He has also written a variety of widely praised young-adult adventure novels. He currently writes the online column Permanent Damage for Comic Book Resources.